Bryan M. Powell

Loving

Miss Bessie

Books by Bryan M. Powell
Christian Fantasy Series
The Witch and the Wise Men
The Lost Medallion
The Last Magi
Journey to Edenstrae

The Jared Russell Series

Sisters of the Veil
Power Play
The Final Countdown

The Chase Newton Series

The Order
The Oath
The Outsider

Non-Fiction/Devotional

Seeing Jesus – A Three Dimensional Look at Worship
Show Us the Father – A 30-Day Devotional
Faith, Family, and a Lot of hard Work – The Grady Gillis Story

Loving

Miss Bessie

To Trish

Happy reading.

By Bryan M. Powell

Christian – Fiction, Southern Humor – Fiction, Georgia – Fiction

Cover design by Bryan M. Powell

Photography by Kevin Tillery – www.kevinleeimages.com

Manufactured in the United States of America

ISBN- 13 – 9781731096197

ISBN- 10 –

Endorsements

I love Miss Bessie ... She reminds me of my Aunt Sammie ... a Staunch Methodist who expected the service to start at precisely at eleven and end at noon..And yes, she dipped Burton..Thanks for the memories Bryan ... you've got a winner here....

Author Mike Ragland
Bertha, and Living with Lucy

Loving Miss Bessie is a refreshing read on the way life used to be in Georgia. Written in a manner that you can visualize, not only the scenery, but also the characters. You can almost taste the sweet tea and feel the gentle Georgia breeze. You can shed a few tears and also laugh out loud with Miss Bessie! Bryan's writing makes the people and places come to life.

Although a work of fiction, every chapter strikes a glimpse of a reality factor for almost everyone.

A great read to bring back a lot of memories in our own lives.

Debbie Ross
Regional Program Coordinator
PO Box 172
Rockmart, GA 30153

I loved reading Loving Miss Bessie so much I read it twice. And yes, I'm in love with Bessie Myers.

Elaine Day
Editor and Chief

Foreword

As you may have guessed, this is a fictional account of a woman whom I created. Some of the stories have real roots, some could have happened and some are totally from my musings. What started as an exercise in creative writing spun out of control as more ideas presented themselves. It all started as Patty and I drove past a dilapidated country home. From there, I began to wonder about the people who lived there. What stories the house held. What secrets, what joys, what laughter, what heartbreaks. I imagined an elderly woman; the last resident to occupy the house and Miss Bessie was created. The house is long gone, so I found one that fits the image I have and so it is with this in mind, I present   to   you   ...   Miss   Bessie.

Meet
Author Bryan M. Powell

Award winning author, novelist and composer Bryan M. Powell is a fulltime author living in Dallas, GA with his wife, Patty, of nearly 50 years. Together they own Hiram Bookstore.

Photography By McC

The Trace O'Reilly Mystery Series – If you are looking for a murder-mystery series, look no further. Built around a young debutant, Lily Peterson, this thriller nearly goes off the rails as things rapidly spin out of control. Were it not for God's intervention and Trace's quick action all would be lost.

Sisters of the Veil – Is a Contemporary thriller ripped off the pages of today's newspaper. Rife with action, adventure and intrigue it is guaranteed to hold your attention and open your eyes to the danger and opportunities all around us.

authorbryanpowell.wordpress.com
authorbryanpowell@gmail.com

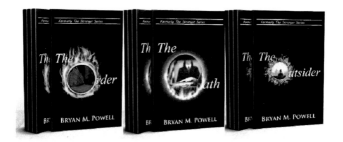

Formerly The Stranger Series – Chase Newton could never have imagined the earth-shattering events which would unfold the day Megan Richards entered his life. Mystery and intrigue are only two words which describe this high-stakes chase across the centuries.

Epic Christian Fantasy Series –

This award winning series is sure to keep you turning the pages as the three wise men learn to adapt to the 21st century. Their epic journey starts when they entrance Jerusalem but quickly spins out of control as they battle the forces of darkness. This is the best example of Spiritual Warfare since Peretti.

Seeing Jesus a Three Dimensional Look at Worship – Seeing Jesus is a thought provoking and compelling expose' on what is true worship.

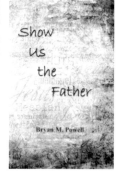

Show Us the Father

Is a thirty-day devotional showing how Jesus demonstrated His Father's character and qualities.

Faith, Family, and a Lot of Hard Work

The Creative Memoirs of Grady E. Gillis as written by Bryan M. Powell

Faith, Family, and a Lot of Hard Work
Born the year the Stock-Market crashed, Mr. Gillis grew up in South Georgia with a 3rd grade education. But by the time he retired, he'd owned 14 companies and the last piece of property he sold was for 1.5 million dollars.

Chapter One

The Present State of Miss Bessie

A few weeks ago, I stopped by the home of my long-time friend, Miss Bessie. That's what she was called by the few folks who still knew her. My sometimes turbulent, sometimes humorous relationship with the elderly saint started not long after I took the pastorate of a small country Methodist church on the outskirts of Albany, Georgia. She seemed to have made it her mission to teach me what my seminary failed to teach. And she was very good at it, I have to admit. Back then, I was as green as a blade of grass. Oh, I could deliver a sermon, but people management, that was a different thing altogether. Lord knows I needed someone to mentor me. I just didn't expect it to be Miss Bessie, but there she was, always ready to 'advise me.' In truth, I didn't mind. Her sometimes pointed, sometimes abrasive guidance was seasoned with an ample dose of love, and for that, I will be eternally grateful.

As I turned the key and shut off the engine, a holy silence settled over the old homestead. A light breeze stirred the Spanish moss which hung lazily in the trees. In the distance, a lonely dove called out its mournful tones.

"Coo, coo, coo."

I stepped from my car and walked the short distance, from where I'd parked underneath a massive live oak, to the porch. With each step, my heels crunched the gravel like some rude child chewing with his mouth open. The porch was lined with clay pots boasting an assortment of Boston ferns, mums, and pansies. I smiled. No one could grow pansies like Miss Bessie. Her green thumb was legendary in these parts.

Putting my foot on the first of three rickety steps, it groaned under my weight but held. The hollow sound of each footstep resonated, but went unnoticed by the spider holding silent vigil over her web clinging to the frame of the unopened door.

My light knocking on Miss Bessie's front door brought the usual response … silence.

I wasn't surprised.

Miss Bessie's hearing had long forsaken her. With care, I pushed the weathered door open; it creaked under its weight and scraped the pine-heart floor like bear claws. A shiver ran the length of my spine, and I shuddered. *It's okay. It's just the door.*

"Miss Bessie?" I called.

Nothing!

Glancing around, I stepped inside. Light from the morning sun filtered through the lace curtains, giving the sitting-room a soft illumination. Particles of dust drifted in lazy circles in and out of the shafts of golden rays which penetrated the yellowed shades.

The pungent aroma of stale coffee, over-ripe fruit, and flowers which had long served their purpose greeted my nostrils.

The aging clock on the mantle no longer beat out its rhythmic cadence. Its two hands were frozen in time. That was the first indication that something wasn't right.

I took a halting breath and knew …

After calling her name and getting the same silent answer, I pushed deeper. I found Miss Bessie on the back porch, sitting in her old rocking chair. To look at her, you would think she was either asleep or in deep prayer. Her hands were folded. Her head bowed. A few strands of grizzled hair, which escaped the hair net that clung to her head like a beehive, hung loosely across her peaceful face. Her tattered Bible lay open on her lap. Gnarled fingers, locked in fervent prayer, sat lightly on its yellowed pages. Across her knees stretched an old, worn quilt. Its raggedy fringes stopped just high enough to reveal her feet, covered with a pair of darned socks. One loosely gathered around her ankle, the other pulled as high as it would go.

One look and I knew.

The worn rocking chair, which had been her support in life,

had become the chariot that had carried her to glory in the small hours of the morning. In some shameful way, I envied her. She had fought the good fight and won the victory. For me, my journey was somewhere between the long dash which marked my birth and the date of my passing. Her journey was now over and we could now fill in the date of her departure.

Miss Bessie had been a turbulent journey. Born the year the stock market crashed, grew up during the Great Depression in South Georgia, married young, lost her only child in childbirth, struggled to make ends meet after the passing of her husband. No, Miss Bessie didn't live a charmed life, but she was a happy soul. She learned early how to make the best out of the worst life handed her. Her godly example was an inspiration to all who met her. It is my prayer that these memoirs, released after her passing, will entertain and inspire you as they have me in writing them.

Her funeral was attended by nearly the entire county. I had no idea the impact she'd made on her community. She will be sorely missed. I preached a simple message of hope and consolation from the tattered Bible I found on her lap. It was as much for me as it was for the standing-room-only crowd which pressed into our small church sanctuary. Amazingly, it was from the very passage she had been reading the day of her passing. The committal service was held not far from the church in a small cemetery. There, we committed her body to the earth next to her husband in hopes of the resurrection of the dead on that glorious morning.

I don't go by Miss Bessie's house anymore. However, rumor has it, if you pass by her former residence about the time the upper branches of the old live oak plays catch with the first rays of sunlight, you might hear Miss Bessie's faint humming as it wafts through the morning air.

If you do, join in. I think she'd like that.

Chapter Two

A Good Chew of Tobacco

The first time I met Miss Bessie was just after I was accepted as the new pastor of Bethel Methodist church, a small congregation located on the outskirts of Albany, Georgia. Having recently graduated from seminary with a divinity degree and having been newly ordained as a Methodist minister, I joined the United Methodist denomination and was assigned here as my first post. I was eager to show this beleaguered church how to step into the twenty-first century. However, it wasn't long before I learned the elderly saints had an, "it-ain't-never- been-done-that-way," approach to doing church.

Needless to say ... it was challenging.

After painting over the name of the previous pastor, I stenciled on my name in its place. By the look and thickness of the layers of paint, I knew I was neither the first nor the last to have his name on this marque. With care, I filled in the letters ... Reverend Timothy Wallace - Pastor. Standing back, I observed my work. Not bad, I mused. I hope it lasts ... the paint-job that is. I had no illusions about my tenure here. By God's grace, I hoped to outlast my predecessor.

As a way of getting better acquainted with my flock, I began visiting each member. I'd heard about Miss Bessie from the others; their "Prayer Requests," left me wondering who needed the prayer. It was not without a measure of anxiety I turned off the highway and drove deeper into the holler where her homestead was located.

I pulled to a stop and stared at the small split-pine cabin resting on wooden posts. It was only later that I learned those posts were Bodark, a very resilient wood imported from Arkansas. The wood was chosen for its durability and toughness, sorta like Miss Bessie. How they got here was a mystery. The house she'd called home, for more years than she'd admit, leaned slightly to one side. The tin roof was littered with pine needles. The sagging stone chimney looked like it might topple over any moment.

It was September, and the summer lingered like a bad dream. Noticing an elderly woman hunched over a black kettle in the backyard, I wondered if Miss Bessie was the reincarnation of the Wicked Witch of the West. I could almost hear her singing, "Bubble, Bubble, Toil and, Trouble."

I got out of my car and took a step in her direction. Startled, she waved me off as if I was trespassing. It never occurred to me to call ahead. The other church folks seemed to have enjoyed my impromptu visits. Apparently, not so with Miss Bessie.

She continued her menacing wave as if swatting at a fly. Then she stood, knocking her wooden chair backward and dashed into the house. Holding my position, I wondered if she'd emerge from the house like Granny Clampett, a double-barreled shotgun clutched in her bony hands ready to pepper me with buckshot.

Moments stretched and finally, her slender form took shape behind the screen door. She pushed it open. It creaked in protest. Then she stepped out; a large jar of peaches in her hands.

"You look skinnier than you did in the newspaper," her craggy voice cut through the morning air.

I looked down at my growing waistline. Concerned their yet unmarried preacher would die of starvation, the ladies of the church started a, "Feed the Hungry," drive with me as their sole benefactor.

Not wanting to get off on the wrong foot, I drew closer, stepped up on the porch and took the proffered jar. "Thank you, kindly," I said, stepping back.

"Care to set a spell?" She stood expectantly, hands gathered in a soiled apron.

I smiled. "Yes, ma'am, I think I will."

She led the way to the backyard where a black kettle sat over a bank of glowing coals. With each puff of wind, they seemed to breathe. I wondered what was in the kettle.

"It's apple butter," she said as if she'd read my mind.

I nodded, not speaking.

Picking up her wooden chair, she glanced in the direction of a shed. "There's another one in there. If you want to stand, that's okay by me, but I have a lot of fessin' up to do. So you might want to sit."

I pinched back a grin, and obeyed. Inside the aging shed was a menagerie of rusting tools. It reminded me of my granddad's garage. The smell of turpentine mingled with paint thinner and pine oil took me back twenty-five years to a boy watching my grandfather sand a board until it was smooth as a baby's bottom.

"You get lost, Preacher?" Her voice caught me between the past and the present.

Sheepishly, I returned, a rickety folding chair in hand. It looked like it had been borrowed from the church, I observed. Maybe that was one of those things she was going to fess-up to.

I took a seat. "Miss Bessie—" I began.

Her gnarled hand shot up like the clown in a Pop-Goes-the-Weasel toy.

"Now Preacher, it's been a spell since I've been in church." She paused to stir the apple butter with a wooden ladle.

I waited. Rumor had it, she caused the last preacher to leave. I braced myself.

"As I was sayin', it's been a while since I've been to church. Ever since my husband passed, it's been hard to get around. My nephew comes and carries me to the grocery store once a week. Other than that, I don't get out much. 'Cassionly one of the church folks would stop by and offer me a ride to church, but ever since the last preacher went to medlin', well ..." Her voice faded and I caught myself leaning in her direction.

Maybe the rumors were true.

"Well, Miss Bessie, I don't plan on—"

She cut me off with a wave. This was her platform and I was her audience. She made that clear with one sweep of her hand.

"Yes, ma'am." I felt like a school-boy.

She continued to share her view of what topics a preacher should preach on, listing salvation and evangelism as her top priority.

"The main thing is to stay out of people's lives. Stick to the Bible and let well enough alone." She concluded with a nod, then stirred the kettle again.

Sensing the conversation was over, I stood to leave.

"Oh, preacher, before you go, there's an envelope on the kitchen table. It's my tithe. Would you mind taking it with you?"

Reluctantly, I walked up the back steps which led into the

house. Inside, the pungent odors of chopped onions and stale coffee assaulted my nostrils. Looking around, I noticed an envelope held down by an old soup can nearly filled with a brown substance, its wrapper long since gone. With care, I slid it aside, lifted the envelope and turned it over. I felt like I was taking the widow's mite and guilt stabbed my heart. Eyeing the brown tobacco stained flap which sealed the envelope, I knew there was one less sermon I needed to prepare.

Chapter Three

Shotgun Shells and Chicken and Dumplin's

"… he was a fine boy, the kind you wouldn't mind your daughter bringing home. That is, if you had a daughter." Miss Bessie's gaze fell on my ringless hand. She paused and took a sip of lemonade, and narrowed her eyes. "Now Preacher, I don't think you've heard a word I said."

I felt my ears burn. She was right. She'd been droning on about her sister's nephew's son ever since we'd sat down on the porch, and my mind wandered—several times.

Two hours earlier, she'd called me. "It's too lovely outside to be cooped up in your office studying Greek tenses," she said, her craggy voice conjuring up wicked images.

Her attempt to pry me from my office worked. Indeed, it was a lovely day. And it didn't take too much persuasion to cause me to close my books and change into something more comfortable. Although sitting with a lonely senior saint was not my idea of how to spend a fall day, apparently, it was God's. So I made the journey into the country. It felt like another country, another era, another world.

It was Bessie Myers' world.

As I strode up to her front porch, I noticed the rays of sunlight piercing the autumn foliage like a thousand javelins. Overhead, a warm breeze drifted through the conifer trees making them sway with a gentle rhythm. In the distance, a Whippoorwill called to the Bob White, who in turn called to the cicada telling it to be quiet. It didn't, and so the lazy afternoon dragged on.

While sitting on her porch, I mopped my brow and took another sip of lemonade letting its cool, tarty flavor soothe my parched throat. My sermon the previous day had left it raw.

It was one of those rare occasions Miss Bessie was in attendance. She sat on the second row, hands gloved, a straw hat perched on her head, and her large print Bible on her lap.

She listened attentively, now it was my turn to listen. I hoped my delivery was not as laborious as hers.

"Have I told you about my late husband? His name was Ned, Ned E. Myers."

Although I was sure she'd told me, I pushed out a weak smile. Shifting in the wicker seat, I said. "Why, no," I lied. I'd confess it later. "Tell me about him."

A distant look filled her eyes and her voice grew light and dreamy. "We were just children back then, so young, so full of life, full of dreams. He'd always wanted to be a doctor, you know. But back then, as it is today, it took money. We barely recovered from the Great Depression, when the Second World War started. His elder brother was drafted and died somewhere in France, leaving him to carry on the family business. So much for his dreams. They were from the holler across the way.

We'd courted off and on for about a year. Then one day he showed up, unannounced, to ask for my daddy for my hand in marriage. That was also the day our mare decided to foal … early. Daddy was plowing the lower forty and momma was in the middle of boiling laundry. That's what we called washing the clothes in those days," she added instructively. "So Ned, who'd read a few medical journals he'd found in the doctor's office, ran to get daddy while I stroked Millie. That's the mare's name," she said, an impish twinkle danced in her eyes.

"I was only fifteen at the time and had never seen a horse in labor. As a matter of fact, I don't recall having seen anything in labor, I mean, giving birth and all." Miss Bessie's cheeks pinked and she fanned herself.

I smiled and took another sip of lemonade.

Seeing my Kerr jar half empty, she took the opportunity to excuse herself. As she disappeared into the house, I saw a double-barreled shotgun leaning against the door frame. Two empty shells lay at odd angles next to its stock.

She returned with a large pitcher of lemonade, its ice cubes bobbing like ships on the sea and I stood out of respect. A light chuckle percolated in her throat as she retook her seat. I couldn't help noticing the tan smear on her lower lip, but I ignored it. We all have our weaknesses, hers was tobacco.

"Such a gentleman, kinda like Ned," she said. With that, she plunged back into her story. "Daddy and Ned rode up on his tractor. Ned jumped off," she grinned. "His foot landed in a pile of cow—" she caught her breath. "Oh my, I almost had a slip of the tongue." Her reference to the 'tongue' didn't escape me as that was the topic of my sermon yesterday. Apparently, it ruffled a few feathers on the prayer chain.

"Anyway," she continued. "Daddy stopped the tractor and followed Ned into the barn to where Millie lay. Her belly was swollen and she seemed to be suffering real bad. I made up my mind right then, if birthin' caused this much pain, I wanted nothin' to do with it. Later I learned the other half of the story and changed my thinkin' … somewhat." She fanned herself vigorously.

"Well, after it was all over we had us a brand new filly," her face beamed as if it happened just yesterday. "Can I impose on you to stay for supper?" All at once, the aroma of chicken and dumplin's wafted from the kitchen. My taste buds went into overdrive.

"That smells mighty good, Miss Bessie, but really you shouldn't have—" A weathered hand cut me off.

"No need to be overly humble, now Preacher. I didn't exactly cook it up for you."

Heat crept up my neck and it was my turn to fan myself. "Oh? Then why did you make chicken and dumplin's, if not for me?"

The lines on her face deepened. She cleared her throat and took a sip of lemonade. Her eyes narrowed into slits as an old blue-tick hound loped across the barren yard. His tongue hung lazily from one side of his mouth and she muttered something about the shotgun, chicken coop, and his cold nose.

It suddenly dawned on me. "Miss Bessie, where's all of your chickens?"

She played with her Kerr jar for a moment before answering.

"You're about to eat them."

Chapter Four

Miss Bessie's Award-Winning, Medicinal Strength, Chicken Soup

For the first time since coming to Albany, I awoke feeling sick. Usually, my physical constitution was resistant enough to ward off most of the germs my small congregation tried to pass along. Not this time.

After taking a mental inventory of my condition, I diagnosed myself with the flu. Upon further consideration, I chided myself for using such a generic term. Admitting I had the flu was like a man confessing he was a sinner. I needed to be more specific. Was it the flu or was it a virus? The way my head and stomach felt, I assumed I was afflicted with a sinus infection and a stomach virus … not the flu. But whatever it was, I knew Miss Bessie had the remedy for it.

The problem was, I lived in the parsonage, an upstairs garage apartment in town, and Miss Bessie lived about seven country miles away. Her occasional visits to purchase supplies and swap gossip, disguised as prayer requests, had gotten less frequent since she'd gotten a telephone.

Rather than risk the long journey into the country to see, "Dr." Bessie, I dialed the number to the only other person I trusted with my health needs. Dr. Wilber Applebee had the unenviable position of being Dougherty county's only doctor and veterinarian. Thus giving him the ability to practice his healing art on both man and beast with impunity. My only fear was that after he'd sampled the local *holy water,* he wouldn't be able to tell the difference between me and a jackass. Although there might be some church members who might dispute that.

Having to wear glasses the thickness of a coke-bottle bottom, to correct his nearsightedness, Dr. Applebee reminded me of Mr. Mc Goo, rather than a family doctor, but I was desperate.

My phone call to the doctor's residence was disappointing. His wife informed me that the good doctor was out at the Fuller's farm delivering a calf. It would be hours before he'd return. Plus, he was on call with the hospital. I saw my chances of a quick recovery go up in a puff of smoke.

The verse, "hope deferred makes the heart grow sick," echoed in my clogged mind.

After taking a fist-full of over-the-counter drugs, I closed my eyes, hoping to sleep off my pounding headache.

No sooner had I drifted off, than my phone jangled. I longed just once to have the liberty to say what was on my mind, but I fought off the temptation. The verse, "be angry and sin not," held my tongue in check.

"Hello," I growled through tangled vocal cords.

"Preacher?"

Why was I not surprised?

"I heard you was sick ..."

"Yes, ma'am. It's my head and stomach.

"Sounds like a sinus infection and stomach virus."

"Now, Miss Bessie, how could you have known that?"

Her craggy voice turned into a gravelly chuckle. "It's a gift."

"I know you have a special gift, but I also know you have a telephone—"

Her chuckle ended abruptly. "Preacher, you wouldn't be suggesting I engaged in the free exchange of contemporary information with my fellow concerned citizens, now would you?"

Despite my throbbing skull, I couldn't suppress a chuckle. "Okay, Miss Bessie, I confess, you have an uncanny gift of discernment, but do you have the ability to prescribe a remedy?"

"Chicken soup," she said without missing a beat.

"Chicken soup?" Her two–word reply took me by surprise.

"Yep, but not just anybody's chicken soup ... 'specially not Doris McClung's. That's liable to make you sicker. No, you need to be on a steady diet of Miss Bessie's award-winning, medicinal strength, chicken soup. It will put hair on your chest, meat on your bones, and health to your soul."

Flopping back on the bed, I adjusted the cool washcloth on my forehead. "That sounds great, but I'm not up to driving out into the country for a bowl of soup."

"If you're sick enough, you will. Remember Esau? When he thought he was going to die, he dragged himself home and bargained with Jacob for a bowl of lentil soup."

"Yes and later wept with bitter tears over the bad deal he made."

Miss Bessie harrumphed. "That may be so, but you have to admit, it must have been a mighty good bowl of stew."

Her logic was inscrutable, but I was in no condition to match wits with her. "Okay, but that still doesn't solve my problem. I can't drive, I'm too sick."

"Well, we'll see to that." The phone clicked and the line went dead.

I had just gotten settled in bed, when I heard someone pounding on the front door. I secretly hoped it was Dr. Applebee … It wasn't.

"Miss Bessie, what a surprise!" I tugged my robe closer around my body to keep out the night chill.

Miss Bessie's face brightened like the dawn over Lake Chehaw. "My nephew, Buford and I were in the neighborhood and thought I'd drop in." The black kettle looked like something out of a fairy tale involving a witch and a red apple.

"What is it?" I inquired even as the aroma of freshly baked cornbread mingled with chicken soup permeated my apartment. Its health restorative qualities had taken effect even before the first spoonful had touched my lips.

A wry smile crinkled the corners of her lips. "Like I said, it's my award-winning, medicinal strength, chicken soup."

She pushed past me and headed to the kitchen. After placing the kettle in the center of my rickety table, she began setting out three bowls and some plates for the cornbread while Buford filled three Kerr jars with iced tea.

My mouth flooded in anticipation of the feast set before us. "If it tastes half as good as it smells, I'd gladly sell my birthright for the receipt."

"It sure beats the medicine I had to take growing up. I remember the time when my brother and I were in middle school, the government started checking us for typhoid, worms, and that sort of stuff. They gave shots and medicine to those who were infected. We'd have to get a sample of our stool, put it in a box, and take them to school. Well, my brother thought he'd be smart and brought in a sample of cow manure. It came back positive. But because my brother was a stout boy, momma and daddy thought the medical staff must have gotten the boxes mixed up, and they made me take my brother's medicine. I knew better, but they refused to believe me. I guess that's what I get for being so ornery," Miss Bessie finished her dialog with a firm nod.

I failed to make the connection, but I knew she was trying to make a point.

Crossing her arms, she leaned against the door frame. "Have I mentioned to you I have a niece who's a better cook than me and she's looking for a good husband?"

All at once, the pain in my head relieved, my sinuses cleared and I could breathe again. "Well, would you look at that, I feel better already. I guess I won't be selling my soul for a bowl of your soup ... or for a wife."

Chapter Five

The Chicken Coop Critter

I only know this story from what Miss Bessie told the other ladies before church began. And since she is not given to exaggeration, or, at least not much, I tend to believe her tale.

It was Sunday morning and I was still in my study with the door cracked open when I heard Miss Bessie's distinctive voice. She tried to whisper, but with her loss of hearing, her whisper was more than the average speaking level. I laid my notes aside and listened … and chuckled.

The story involved an unwanted visitor to her chicken coop. The one other time she had a disturbance in her chicken coop, ended with her having an abundance of chicken and dumplings.

Sitting in her usual pew, she began. "The other night I was about to turn when I heard a ruckus in the chicken coop. Not wanting Ole Blue to cold-nose me, again, I tied him to a rope on the porch. Once I was sure he wouldn't cause me no trouble, I slipped on my clodhoppers so's I didn't step on any surprises, grabbed my shotgun and flashlight, and made my way across the yard to the coop. The moon was full, makin' the yard glow in a bluish haze. My breath came in short, ghost-like puffs in the cool night air, and I clutched my robe tighter to keep out the chill.

The chickens were makin' such a racket that I dared not enter without first sayin' a prayer and takin' a big gulp of air. For all I knew, Burster, the rooster, was having a heyday with his hens. That bein' the case, I was not much interested in disturbin' him.

Then I heard an unfamiliar sound. It was a cross between a growl and a whimper. I figured whatever it was, it was takin' a beatin' from the hens. I considered just staying outside until the fight was over, but then something landed hard against the hen house wall. It struck with such force that it nearly set me on my fanny," she said, making sure she didn't use any coarse language in God's house.

She continued. "One hand holding the shotgun, I held the flashlight with the other hand and carefully lifted the latch. All at once, the door flew open and chickens fluttered out as if they were chased by a demon. It was all I could do to keep from shootin' every one of them. I stood panting, wondering what in Sam Hill caused such a stampede.

I fought the urge to sneeze. Whatever was in the coop had given me and the chickens such a fright that my heart stuttered in my chest.

Taking a shaky step, I peered inside the coop and swung the beam of light around. Chicken feathers hung in the air reminding me of the time my sister and I got into a pillow fight. One of the pillows ripped open, letting a thousand feathers flutter out. We laughed into the night, but then Daddy came in and whooped us both, but I digress.

After waiting for my pulse to slow, I began to search for the cause of the mayhem. My breath caught in my throat as a pair of beady eyes stared back at me. A moment later, a streak of black with two white stripes scampered between my feet, making me leap like I'd been cold-nosed by Ole' Blue again.

Gulping air, I pointed the shotgun and prepared to squeeze the trigger when I remembered what happened when Daddy shot a skunk. It took him days to get the stink off.

I knew the supply of eggs had declined of recent but I never considered a thieving skunk to be the culprit. Now I knew, but how to stop the varmint from returning became my newest challenge.

I recalled Daddy telling me about a similar problem. He said he stopped the unwanted guest from returning by spreading fox-pee-laced dirt inside and outside the chicken coop.

That posed another problem. Where would I find dirt soiled by a fox?

The Bible verse about the little foxes spoiling the grapes came to mind and I thought about it a spell. Where on earth am I going to find grapes in these hills? At one time, my daddy had a small grape arbor, but that had long since fallen into neglect.

With the night pressing in around me and the skeeters buzzing around my ears, I decided to take this up in the morning. So I shooed the chickens back into their coop and slammed the door shut. Knowing the fox would probably return, I decided to spend the rest of the night, keeping vigil over my prized possessions. Rather than get eaten alive by those pesky mosquitoes, I found a pot of dried sweet grass and lit it on fire. It did the trick for a while, but it left me feeling a bit tipsy. It was either suffer a slow death by a thousand mosquito bites or feeling woozy, I chose woozy. After rummaging around in the shed, I found four more pots of the weed and resumed my vigil.

About the time the sun announced the day, I couldn't care less about my chickens. I wobbled into my house and dumped half a can of coffee into the percolator and turned it on. It was nearly noon when my head cleared. I decided right then, no more sweet grass. Frm now on, I'd get me some citronella and stay inside as far away from those pesky bugs as possible. But first, I had one more thing to do. I had to get me some fox-dirt.

Chapter Six

Of Skunks and False Teachers

I was as interested in knowing how Miss Bessie got rid of the skunk as the rest of the church, but I had a sermon to deliver. With due diligence, I cleared my throat and interrupted her story. After enduring a few groans, I called the service to order with a few hymns.

The congregation meekly followed my lead as we went through our morning liturgy, but in the back of my mind, I knew they were half listening, half wishing I'd end the sermon so they could get back to Miss Bessie's story.

So did I, for that matter.

I did my best to make application to Miss Bessie's plight, but it fell on deaf ears. With a final "Amen," I closed my Bible, removed my liturgical robe, and hung it up. By then, Miss Bessie had resumed her tale. I eased into a pew, my interest growing by the second.

"There was a skunk out there that needed to learn a lesson," she said, "and it was my responsibility to teach it. I headed to where I last saw the fox. The path led deep into the woods, which by then was getting dark. That was when my flashlight batteries decided to fade. But I was determined to win this battle," she shifted and glanced at me. An impish twinkle danced in her eyes.

"It was either him or me. Halfway down the path leading to the lake, I stumbled over an ornery root outcropping and landed on my hands and knees. The flashlight skittered in one direction and my shotgun in another. For a moment, all I could do was to push myself up on my hands and knees and peer into the darkness. Wishing I wasn't so stubborn, I forced my legs under me and stood. I leaned against a knotty pine and waited for my heart rate to return to normal.

Rustling in the bushes, however, convinced me that staying where I was, wasn't a good idea. As I brushed myself off, I noticed a distinct smell. 'Fox-pee.' I whispered. I stumbled right into a freshly anointed mound of dirt getting it on my night-shirt. In the darkness, I scooped up as much of the smelly dirt as I could and dumped it into a leaky bucket. Then I picked my way back up the path.

Overhead, the moon jeered at me as if he was enjoying the spectacle. I looked a sight ... an old woman, my straggly hair hanging across my face, and my nightshirt soiled with smelly dirt. Shafts of silver rays cut through the leafy ceiling pointing at me like I was a criminal, and maybe I was. I'd taken something from the forest without giving something back. Right then, I determined to refill the hole with dirt from my flower bed. The thought seemed quite absurd, but at the time, it made sense.

By the time I'd reached the chicken coop, the hens had gathered on their perches and were clucking softly. It reminded me of a gaggle of old women talking about last Sunday's sermon or the new UPS delivery man who'd shown up at Martha Dooley's doorstep the other day. I took a step inside, being careful not to step on a wayward chick.

No sooner had I started to sprinkle the dirt, than the chickens rose in such a flutter, that my heart nearly leaped from my body. They began flapping and pecking at each other, then they turned on me. We rushed from the coop like it was on fire.

Leaning over, hands on my knees, I considered my actions. I guess the fox-pee-dirt must have upset the ladies. Not wanting a repeat performance, I decided to head to the house, but halfway up the steps, Ole Blue got a whiff of my scent, and lunged at me. His rope broke and he landed on top of me, snarling like the hound of the Baskervilles. Fearing for my life, I shucked off the fox-pee-covered nightshirt and let him have it. Within minutes, he'd torn it to shreds.

Except for my bloomers, I lay bare naked, shivering in the night air. Not wanting to catch a cold, I struggled to my feet and dashed into my house only to find I'd left the back door open. A chill filled the room, but that wasn't what made my skin crawl. A pair of beady eyes stared at me. Mr. Skunk decided to pay me a visit and this time, he left his calling card.

Forgetting I was naked as a jaybird, I lit out of the house before getting skunked. Fortunately, earlier that day, I'd hung a load of wash on the line. At least, I was able to clothe myself. After my breathing calmed, I found the bucket of fox-pee-dirt. Covering my mouth and nose with a hankie soaked with vanilla, which I'd gotten from the kitchen, I slinked into the livin' room where Mr. Skunk huddled in the corner. I'd hoped by now he would have departed, but I s'pose he liked my home as much as I did. Although, with his recent emission, I liked it somewhat less. But I was in a quandary, either my home was going to smell like a skunk, or it was going to smell like fox-pee.

Neither seemed too appealing.

So I took a chance on doing the unorthodox. I sat down on my rocker and began to hum. Knowing I was unable to carry a tune in a bucket, especially one filled with fox-pee laden dirt, I knew I had at least a fifty-fifty chance of sending the varmint skittering, so I kept humming.

Directly, the four-footed bandit gave me a quizzical look and scampered out the door where Ole Blue waited. Having expended his spray earlier, Mr. Skunk was unable to mount a decent defense and had to retreat into a thicket. Blue tried to give him chase, but catching a whiff of the critter's stink, he decided to call off the chase."

After finishing her tale, Miss Bessie sat back and sighed. "It kinda reminds me of what you have to put up with, Preacher."

It was my turn to give Miss Bessie a quizzical look. "Miss Bessie, I'm afraid I'm not following you."

She snickered. "No, I don't s'pose you would. You see, havin' a skunk in the hen house is like havin' a false teacher in the church. Sometimes you have to resort to unorthodox methods to rid yourself of the varmint before he causes a big stink."

I sat bolt straight. Miss Bessie had an uncanny way of pointing out a matter I'd been dealing with for the last several months. We had allowed a man to join our assembly who claimed to be a Bible scholar. As needy as we were to have biblically grounded teachers, we moved to accept him without checking his credentials; that decision proved to be a big mistake. Using his position, Dr. Morehouse began to question the doctrine of the Second Coming claiming if Jesus ever did return, he would do it sometime in the middle of the tribulation. To further confuse folks, he claimed the tribulation was already upon us.

"What do you suggest we do?" I asked.

Putting a finger to her chin, Miss Bessie gave me a wan smile, and I knew she had a plan. "Well, you could start by delivering a series of fiery sermons from second Thessalonians."

I'd already considered that, but by her tone, I knew she had one other suggestion. "And?"

An impish twinkle danced in her eyes. "You could schedule me to sing, "When We All Get to Heaven."

She leaned back and began to hum a barely recognizable rendition of the old favorite.

"You know, I think you may have the answer …"

Chapter Seven

Happy Birthday

I'm not quite sure if it was to make amends for the mess she made by singing *When We All Get to Heaven* or her comments there afterwards. But Miss Bessie's timing couldn't have been worse.

As it turned out, Dr. Morehouse, the gentlemen who'd been questioning our position on the Second Coming, happened to be out of town the service when I scheduled Miss Bessie to sing. Her comments afterward fell on mostly deaf ears ... literally. It didn't help that I'd killed her microphone and our hearing impaired folks sat stock-still, watching her mouth move but not actually hearing her. Those who did hear her, however, made sure Dr. Morehouse and everyone else knew Miss Bessie had spoken.

By mid-afternoon the following day my phone was ringing off the hook. At least it was ringing. I remembered the old adage, 'All advertising is good advertising,' and smiled.

But I digress …

The following Sunday, Miss Bessie sprang a surprise birthday party after the evening service. The problem was … it wasn't my birthday. I could hardly complain, however. The fellowship was encouraging and the cake she'd baked was out of this world. It was a double-chocolate cake with rich, chocolatey icing. Were it not for me getting the first slice, I would not have gotten one. It literally melted in my mouth. Apparently, her baking skills were as notable as her award-winning, medicinal strength, chicken soup.

It was only after we'd eaten the cake that I informed her and the congregation that my birthday was actually the following month on the twenty-seventh.

Undaunted, Miss Bessie insisted they plan a big celebration … one for the sudden departure of Dr. Morehouse and my thirtieth birthday. Although I had to remain silent concerning the loss of a church member, I secretly rejoiced.

Forcing to keep a straight face, I dismissed the group and returned home with visions of chocolate cake dancing in my head.

Fortunately, the month passed without any further outbursts from Miss Bessie. Looking at the attendance report, I breathed a sigh of relief as our attendance reached a new high. I wasn't sure if it was related to the flap over Dr. Morehouse or Miss Bessie's comments. But for whatever reason, our attendance was moving in the right direction.

I make mention of this fact only to set in context the tenuous position I held with the convention. Since coming to Bethel Methodist Church, our attendance had flagged. Sickness, the passing of some of our elderly, and a general disinterest in spiritual matters all contributed to a smaller congregation.

As I understand it, there was a, seldom mentioned, condition in my contract requiring me to report steady growth and to fail to do so could jeopardize my standing with the Church-Growth and World Evangelism Committee.

Reporting an increase in attendance over last month brought a smile to my director's face and an 'Atta boy, well-done.' His verbal pat on the back, bolstered my confidence, though for the life of me, I couldn't put my finger on why.

And so it was with renewed energy I plunged into the new month, forgetting about my birthday party.

When the last Sunday rolled around, I knew something was afoot. Small clusters of people gathered speaking in hushed voices. Their averted glances and stifled chuckles only heightened my anxiety. Were they plotting to vote me out or raise my salary?

I couldn't tell.

Hard as I tried, I couldn't remember the point of my sermon. My mind was captivated by one of the visitors sitting midway down the aisle. It was only later I learned her name was Iris Ashcroft, the Baptist minister's daughter. Why she was visiting a

Methodist church and why that night was a mystery. I tried to blame it on my oratorical delivery, but I knew better. Her presence caused just enough stir among the congregation that I wondered if they would remember the point of my message as well.

Mercifully, I brought the message to an end and called on the head deacon to close the service. To my surprise, he stood and blessed the food we were about to partake of and then I remembered. It was my birthday.

It wasn't hard for me to act surprised as it had totally slipped my mind. With no family close by and no one to celebrate the occasion, I had little interest in going out to a restaurant and eating alone. I did that most of the time.

I had called the local pizza shop so many times I had the number memorized and they knew what I wanted without me saying it. Such were the benefits of a small town with one pizza joint.

So it was with minimal resistance, I allowed myself to be guided to the lower level, which, along with our Sunday School, held the Fellowship Hall. It was decorated in festive ribbons and bulging, colorful balloons. To my relief, the tangy scent of sulfur from recently lit matches and the aroma of freshly brewed coffee masked the musty odor which lingered in the subterranean space.

I had planned on bringing the matter up at the next business meeting, but finances and typical deacon foot-dragging kept it off the table for discussion.

Standing at the back of the serving line was Iris; her blue eyes seemed to dance in the glow of thirty candles. The overhead fluorescent light encircled her blond hair with a soft glow giving her an angelic appearance. I hoped she didn't look too closely at the number of candles. By my count, she couldn't have been over twenty-five, but who was I to judge a woman's age.

As pastor, I felt it my duty to introduce myself and collect as much information as I could about our guest. With my iPad in hand, I secretly hoped she'd be impressed with our technology. She was, or at least she was gracious enough to act impressed. For the next fifteen minutes, I probed her background, trying to establish some common ground between a Methodist minister and a Baptist preacher's daughter. To my delight, I found we had quite a bit of commonality between us. Immediately, a plan began to form in my mind on how to establish a beachhead on that ground.

I made a mental note of her birth year and was in the middle of doing some quick calculating when I heard my name called.

Looking up, I saw my head deacon moving toward me with deliberation. He snagged my elbow and dragged me to the center of the room while Iris stifled a snicker. My face heated and I hoped it wasn't too obvious that I'd held the serving line up.

It was Miss Bessie, who greeted me with an over-stuffed plate brimming with a large portion of green bean casserole, macaroni and cheese, several chicken legs, a couple of deviled eggs and sweet potato soufflé'. It took both hands to carry it to the table. Someone handed me a plastic cup of sweet tea, which I took gratefully.

Having that much attention lavished on me was a bit heady. As a young pastor, I had not yet learned how to gratuitously receive compliments and envelopes stuffed with wrinkled ones and fives. But I was learning.

I was mid-way through the mountain of food, when Iris plopped down across from me. Apparently, the Baptists had no qualms about the size of their plates either. Hers was heaped with whatever was not on my plate and I fought the urge to ask her for a slice of ham, which hung off the edge of her plate like Ole Blue's tongue. She must have seen me eyeing it because she took her plastic knife, whacked off a chunk and forked it in my direction.

"I'll trade you a slice of ham for a fork full of green bean casserole," she said. She dangled it playfully in front of me like a red flag.

"Thanks," I said, offering her a warm smile.

I took the fork from her hand, allowing my fingers to glide across the back of her hand. It was smooth as butter.

Without taking my eyes off her, I shoved the meat in my mouth and chewed it thoughtfully. It was a good trade. The ham was moist and slightly salty.

I was about to ask her for another slice when the church family drew a circle around me and began an off-tune rendition of Happy Birthday.

Again, my face heated, but what was I to do? It was my birthday, though I had little to do with the where, when and how of the matter.

After the song subsided, the crowd parted letting Miss Bessie enter with a large slice of cake. It wasn't her famous chocolate cake, but it looked equally delicious. She set it down next to my elbow and the church family grew quiet.

"Take a bite, Preacher," she said, giving my forearm a slight nudge.

I felt a slight quiver of concern run down my back as all eyes were riveted on me. The air seemed to be filled with electricity. Expectation, anticipation, a giddy glee hung in the air like the smoke of a dozen chimneys.

"Well, if it's half as good as the chocolate cake you made, I'd like to reserve a second piece for later."

"I'm sure that can be arranged, Preacher," she said with a wry smile tugging the corners of her mouth. "Now, eat up."

Another nudge.

Another quiver of concern.

I couldn't shake the feeling I'd been set up, but with Iris sitting expectantly across from me, it was too late to back out.

Lifting my fork, I plunged it into the center and brought it to my lips. My taste buds rippled with anticipation.

I opened my mouth and jammed the fork in. Immediately, my eyes began to water, the air rushed from my lungs and my throat felt like it had been set afire.

Gasping for oxygen, and barely able to see straight, I grasped for the cup of tea. It danced from my fingers and tipped over. A second later the brownish liquid spread across the plastic table cloth like the closing of the Red Sea.

It took all my fortitude to force air into my lungs.

Laughter rang in my ears.

The faces of my normally restrained congregation were bleeding tears.

"What was in that cake?" I sputtered.

An impish smile spread across Miss Bessie's face. "That, Preacher, was my world-famous spice cake."

After taking a gulp of tea, I forced the question, "Miss Bessie, what was it spiced with?"

The crowd roared with laughter.

"Well, Preacher, to be honest … it's Brandy."

I felt my chance of building a relationship with Iris sink like the Titanic.

To my surprise, she snatched up my fork and stabbed it into the meaty center. Before I could stop her, she jammed it into her mouth.

I expected watering eyes, gasping lungs, and sputtering.

Nothing.

It was Miss Bessie, who broke the wire-tight atmosphere. "Well, Preacher. You may have found a kindred spirit."

Chapter Eight

Trick or Treat

October 31st was a particularly frightful night, especially if you found yourself walking the lonely dirt road leading to Miss Bessie's house.

Rumors of strange sightings in the vicinity emerged, and by the time they reached the middle school, they had grown to legendary proportions. Why someone would tread the narrow lane after dark was a mystery, but tread they did.

Three twelve-year-old boys, dressed in hero costumes carrying grocery sacks filled with an assortment of cellophane wrapped candies, made the yearly journey. Call it a dare, a rite of passage, or just plain orneriness, they were not coming for a handout ... they were on a mission. With each tentative step, the more fearful the pale-faced boys became. The forest, now stripped of its foliage, reached out in long, spider-like fingers. Deep shadows edged the road. The barren trees swayed and groaned their warnings not to proceed.

They didn't listen.

Snap!

Something deep in the woods moved. A guttural snort, followed by a grunt sent shiver-flesh over the boys' skin. Stifling their cries, the boys skittered back ten feet and waited for whatever it was to leave. No sooner had the boys taken another step when a shadow leaped from behind a bush and splayed across the road.

Voices from the paved road called to them to return, yet the boys pressed on.

Finally, the shaken trio emerged from the shadowed protection of the woods into a wide clearing. Behind them, the forest creaked and moaned. Ahead, lay Miss Bessie's yard veiled in soft tones. A wispy cloud paused over the moon's face temporally darkening the scene. After a moment, it cleared. Gilded light returned, causing blackened shapes to dance like skeletons across the lawn. An oak tree, void of its leaves, scraped its cat-like limbs against Miss Bessie's tin roof as if it were seeking a flea. Not too far away, the ever-questioning hoot-owl asked who it was who ventured thus far without his permission.

"Who? Who?" he asked.

No one answered.

A craggy chuckle broke the pervading silence. The boys froze in their tracks. Eyes wide as stopwatches, they peered into the yellowed night. One boy bolted. His frightened cries echoed through the trees as he scampered over log and limb. Something large leaped from the porch with a clatter and gave chase. In an instant, the remaining two boys scattered. One dashed back down the road from whence he came, the other dove for the cover of a large oak tree.

Panting, the one boy hiding behind the tree, waited for his breathing to slow and his heart rate to return to normal. Hands slick, he gripped the rugged bark and leaned around the massive trunk to take a peek at what or who it was that made the frightening sound.

There she was ... a woman, dressed in a dark robe, leaning over a large black cauldron. Her gnarled knuckles glowed white in the dim illumination as she gripped the handle of a ladle and stirred something. A gray wisp of steam emanated from the pot and quickly disappeared like a phantom in the night. From his vantage point, he could hear the woman humming. The tune was indiscernible, and even if he could, he had no interest in asking her to sing in church the next Sunday.

"What are you looking at, boy?" The woman's voice crackled like the fire beneath the cauldron.

Knowing it was too late to run, not to mention the fact that he promised his buddies he'd take a picture of the witch if she didn't kill him with her steely eyes, the boy fingered his cell phone and pushed the camera mode.

"Nottin', ma'am."

"Then come out from behind that tree and show yourself."

Knees knocking, the boy pushed himself away from the tree and stepped into the golden moonlight. His breath came in short puffs of condensation as he tried to maintain control of his bladder. After all, what good would it do him if he took the picture at the cost of wetting his britches? He would never live it down.

"Come closer."

It was too late. It was all or nothing. Taking a final gulp of air, he began to walk. The wet grass soaked through the thin exterior of his tattered sneakers, but he kept walking. Something soft and squishy oozed from beneath his foot, and he hoped it wasn't what he thought it was. It was as if his legs were commanded by the woman's voice, not his mind. Or was she in his head; commanding, demanding, controlling his every movement? Stiff-legged, the boy moved within ten feet of the cauldron and stopped.

"There now, that wasn't so bad ... was it?" Miss Bessie's voice was as gravelly as an old smoker's.

By now, the boy's mouth felt like a creek-bed in the middle of the summer. Forcing a dry swallow, he commanded his tongue to come unstuck from the roof of his mouth. "Yes, ma'am, I mean ... no ... I mean—"

"Stop stuttering, boy. I'm not going to bite you."

All at once, Ole Blue came prancing from the shadows; his ears flopping, his tongue lapping the goop which hung from the corners of his mouth.

"But he might," her voice crackled as the dog pounced on the stricken boy's shoulders.

Shaken, the youth let out a blood-curdling cry, dropped his phone, and sprinted for the woods with the hound baying after him.

Within minutes, the boy's cries filled the forest as Ole Blue gave chase. As the voices faded, Miss Bessie gave the apple butter, one last stir and chuckled.

"Works every time."

Reaching down, she fingered the boy's phone. It was an older version similar to the one she'd had before she dropped it into the bowels of her outhouse. She pressed a button and suddenly saw herself. She lifted her chin, smiled and touched the screen. Momentarily blinded by the bright flash, it fell from her fingers into the grass with a soft thud.

After a few moments, her eyes readjusted, and she picked it up again. Using what little she knew about it, she pressed the screen, chose send and smiled.

"The boy will get a kick out of his foray, but he'll have to come back here to get his phone," she said to herself. Then she slid it into her pocket, patted it and chuckled. Within minutes, another group of children giggled nervously as they made their way down her lane.

Yes, indeed, it was a particularly frightful night.

Chapter Nine

The Still

It had been a quiet morning until the morning's silence was broken by the warble of the town's only fire truck. It sped past me belching black smoke like a locomotive. A moment later, an aging ambulance limped along trying its best to keep up. No sooner had the dust settled than a black and white police car stormed around the corner and sped off in the same direction. It was the most activity our little town had seen since the New Year's celebration. "This will make headline news," I chuckled as I reached the church office.

After tossing my keys on the counter, my police scanner sprang to life. As a way of ministering to the community, I had one installed and was on call for any medical emergencies. I snatched up the receiver. "Hello?!"

"Pastor Wallace? This is Chief Parker."

I waited as he paused to respond to someone's question, before returning to the phone. Clearing his throat nervously, he continued, "Sir, there's been an accident out at the Myer's place."

My breath froze. "That's Miss Bessie's place."

"Yes, sir," the fire chief replied succinctly.

Mind racing, I forced out the obvious question. "Chief Parker, what happened? Is Miss Bessie all right?"

A pause further escalated my concern. "As I said, there's been an accident. Miss Bessie's okay, but she's a bit shook-up and she's asking for you."

"What kind of accident?" I asked, grabbing my coat and clerical collar before dashing out the door.

Another pregnant pause heightened my anxiety. "Well, sir, it's kind of a sensitive matter. It seems the police are involved and they cautioned me not to say too much over an open channel. But she's asking for you, so I recommend you hightail it out here el quick-o, if you know what I mean."

"I'm leaving now. Should I come to the hospital?"

"No, sir. Like I said, she's okay." He released a gruff laugh and added. "You know Miss Bessie, even if she was missing a limb, she'd fight like a bobcat in a pond if you tried to take her to the hospital."

I had to agree.

I sent up a quick prayer for Miss Bessie's safety as I raced out of town like a bat out of Hades. By the time I arrived, the ambulance and fire truck had gone. Only the sheriff in his black and white police car remained.

Deep tire tracks led around to the back of Miss Bessie's house and ended near a smoldering pile of wood and twisted metal. Gray smoke filtered through the trees and lingered like a bad attitude. After parking my car under the shade of the large pin oak, I got out and glanced around. A pungent smell permeated the air, making me wonder what had happened. Shaking off the feeling of dread, I padded across her barren yard. From a distance, I could see into the house where two figures moved like unhappy spirits.

"This is not good," I muttered.

As I approached, I heard a low conversation spilling out. Pausing, I tried to eavesdrop, hoping to learn the nature of the sudden distress call.

"You sure no one else was around when it blew?" It was the police chief's gruff voice.

I had only met him once. It was just after I'd moved to town and I'd parked in a handicapped parking slot near the entrance of the hospital since I hadn't gotten my Pastoral Parking Permit. Even though my old clunker bore a handicapped license plate, I lacked the blue Parking Permit. As I returned from making a hospital visit, the sheriff greeted me with a ticket and a toothy smile.

"Here you go, Pastor. This may not be a big city like you're from, but we here in small town USA don't take too kindly to city slickers takin' up the handicapped parking slots. Get yourself a parking permit and park in the designated slot reserved for clergy next time."

He wheeled around and trudged off. A week later, my wallet was thirty dollars lighter. I just hoped the offerings rebounded to cover my hospital visit.

It was with these musings; I stood and listened to the ongoing conversation.

"Yep, I was just comin' back to check on it when kabang. Fire, wood, and tin exploded all around me. I was lucky I didn't get blown to bits as well."

A low chuckle emanated from the sheriff before continuing. "Well, it sure is a shame. You make the best cider in the county. A lot of folks will have to go elsewhere for their elixir of joy."

Cider? Elixir of Joy? My mind raced. *What in the world was he talking about? Surely this Godly saint wouldn't be involved in making—*

"Preacher?" Miss Bessie's raggedy voice yanked me to attention. "I know you're out there listening. You might as well come in and check on me."

I stifled a laugh as I climbed the rickety steps and entered Miss Bessie's living room. I found her sitting on a rumpled couch with the sheriff holding her hand and kneeling in front of her as if he were her suitor about to confess his love. The sight was comical were it not for the black smudges marking her weathered features.

A mantle of sobriety suddenly enveloped me and I nodded to the happy couple. "I see you have everything under control, Sheriff. Maybe I should leave you two alone a little longer."

The sheriff's eyes bulged and his face reddened, while Miss Bessie fanned herself with a hanky. "Now Preacher, he was just being kind. Weren't you Sheriff?" an impish twinkle danced in her eyes.

Standing, the flustered officer, cleared his throat and glanced down at her. "Yes, ma'am."

"We're just glad you're okay, but it's too bad about your still." Giving me a sharp stare, he continued, "Maybe you should try turning some spring water into wine before next communion. That would make a lot of people happy … heck, it might even grow your little congregation." His comment stung like a sliver between the toes, but I bit my tongue.

Stepping through the front door, the sheriff disappeared without further comment. I waited until I heard the car door shut before turning my attention to Miss Bessie.

"So tell me, Miss Bessie, what happened?"

Fingering her apron nervously, she took a quick glance over her shoulder. "I, I have a bit of a confession to make."

I waited, knowing already what was coming.

"You see Preacher, we country folk have our own way of doing things. You'll learn that soon enough if you stay around for very long."

I took that as a subtle hint what not to preach against. My list was growing. Lowering myself into the chair across from her, I waited for the full confession.

After a moment, she rose to her feet and began pacing. "I know the good Book talks against strong drink, but we here in the holler never took that literally."

The slight tremble in her voice betrayed her normally calm exterior. "Anyway, didn't the Apostle Paul tell his preacher boy to drink a little wine for his stomach's sake?"

This was not the confession I expected. It was more like an apologetics lesson on drinking rather than an admission of guilt, I mused.

"Yes, ma'am, he did, but I don't think Paul was talking about white-lightening."

She stopped mid-stride, her thumb and forefinger clutching her stubbly chin. "That may be so, but that's beside the point. A lot of folk 'round here have come to appreciate quality when it comes to their libation."

Knowing my synod took a more liberal stance on drinking, I

was reluctant to come down too hard on the dear woman. Especially since by the looks of her, and the smoldering pile of wreckage out back, which had been her still, it was a moot point. I wondered if it weren't an act of God, but resisted the temptation to bring it up. "So what are you confessing, Miss Bessie?" I asked, trying to get the conversation back on track.

She smiled, lifted another tithe envelope from the mantle and handed it to me. It bore the same brown smudge as the one I'd retrieved the last time I was here. "You know I'm a woman on a fixed income."

"Yes, ma'am."

"And that I don't get much from the guverment."

I nodded.

"Well, seein's I don't have much by way of worldly means, I augment my income by sellin' my little concoction to the locals. What with my still destroyed, I won't be able to tithe like I used to."

She let the impact of her statement have its full effect.

"So you might consider takin' the sheriff's suggestion . . . Just sayin'."

Chapter Ten

Confessions and Lessons

The following day, after the still blew up, I went to check on Miss Bessie only to find the doctor had paid her a visit and insisted she go to the hospital for tests. I would have liked to have heard her reaction and pitied the poor doctor. Getting her to do anything she didn't want to do was like trying to motivate an old mule.

That reminded me of a story she told me. They owned a mule, which they used to plow the corn and potato fields. One day, the mule refused to go down the furrow. Instead, it stomped across the furrows and made a mess of things, so she gave it a whipping. All that did was confuse the animal. The moral of the story was, you can't beat a mule into doing anything it doesn't want to do. "It's kinda like church folk," she added.

I thought of Miss Bessie.

When I arrived at the hospital, I found Miss Bessie in a talkative mood. She was encircled by a gaggle of nurses and she was saying, "When the Depression hit, my family lost everything; their savings, their land, daddy's job. It was bad. We had to move in with my grandparents on daddy's side for a short time. That was a bit of a bumpy road. Times were hard. My parents and grandparents only owned one vehicle between them and it was a truck. They used that vehicle for everything, even hauling farmhands around. After a while, my grandpa thought it best for the family if we moved out. Daddy didn't know much about farming, but he was about to learn." She laughed at the memory.

"My grandmother on momma's side owned a farm on Salt Lick Road and couldn't handle it. So we moved by mule and wagon since the truck was out of commission at the time. At least that's what grandpa said. That wasn't so bad since we didn't have that much to move anyway. Out of nowhere my uncle drove up and honked the horn. It nearly scared the mule to death. That made a big impression on me because that was the first time I'd ever seen a car.

"Back then, before you could move in, you had to scald the walls and floor with hot water because almost every house had bedbugs. We moved in late December and had to boil water in a kettle in the yard. Then daddy would throw the water on the ceiling and walls, but it would freeze before it got to the floor. So we had to wait until the weather warmed before we could finish."

It appeared to me, the nurses had nothing better to do than listen to the elderly woman's storytelling and I was not about to interrupt her. She caught a glimpse of me and nodded. "Nice of you to show up, Preacher, I was just saying, one of the funniest things I ever saw happened the year we had an ice storm. The ground was iced over and we had to use an ax to cut a pathway to the barn so momma could get to the cows to milk them. What was so funny was when daddy tried to feed the chickens. When they came out of the coop, they started sliding across the ice trying to get the corn. We laughed until our sides hurt. Have you ever laughed that hard, Preacher?"

I felt my face heat. I had to admit, I'd never laughed that hard.

"Maybe you should," she admonished.

Point taken.

A buzzer sounded and the nurses scattered like a bevy of quail leaving just me and Miss Bessie. The interruption didn't seem to faze her.

"Growing up, I was pretty ornery. I wasn't about to let anybody boss me around. My aunt caught me spittin' into the well. She said, 'You better get away. I am going to tell your daddy, and he is going to whip you.' I gave her a devilish grin and spit in it again and ran.

When daddy got home, my aunt told on me. Daddy really cracked the whip. I got the point that I needed to obey my elders. After that, I didn't spit in the well ever again."

I knew I wasn't the perfect child, but I wasn't about to make that confession to Miss Bessie or the whole prayer chain would soon be a buzz.

She pressed ahead without taking a breath. This was the most confessing she'd done since we'd first met. "Later that spring we'd eaten most of our supplies, and we were getting pretty hungry. We had no flour for biscuits, so we had to take corn to the mill and have it ground into cornmeal. One day I was so hungry that I climbed up a tree and ate a green pear. It made me so sick, I, well, you get the idea. When momma found out, she took a tea weed and put it on me. Back in those days, that was the main way they disciplined us, kids. It hurt really bad, but it didn't draw blood."

I nodded.

"I hope when you finally do get married and have children you won't use a tea weed to discipline them," she said matter-a-factly.

Our confession and child-rearing lesson ended as abruptly as it started.

"Have I told you the story about getting my first pair of shoes?" Miss Bessie's question interrupted my thoughts.

"No, I don't think so." I knew even if she did, she'd insist on telling me.

She began, "I was somewhere around five or six when my aunt

and uncle stopped by my house in their new Edsel. They were from the upper side of the railroad; if you know what I mean … snooty is what momma called them."

I smiled.

She continued. "I was in the yard playing with the chickens. Actually, I was trying to catch them, but you know how hard that is. Anyway, they asked momma if they could carry me to town, they wanted to do something nice for me. She agreed but told me to behave. I agreed and climbed in the back seat. I'd never been inside a car before and I was so excited. When we got to town they stopped in front of the Five and Dime. That was a variety store offering a wide assortment of cheap items," she said instructively.

I knew what they were. We called them Seven-Elevens.

I heard her in the background.

"They bought me a whole bag of candy and I ate so much it made me sick." She chuckled at the memory.

So did I.

"Anyway, while we were in town, they took me to a store called Buster Brown and bought me a pair of shoes. It was the first pair I'd ever owned and I was so proud of them. When I got home, I walked in circles just to see what kind of tracks they'd make. I wore those shoes to church and school until I'd worn holes in the soles." she laughed at her rhyme.

She eyed my recently purchased loafers.

Not to be outdone, I called to mind my own childhood memory. "When I was a kid, I had a pretty bad habit of sucking my thumb. My parents tried everything to get me to stop, but nothing helped. One day, my mother was working in the kitchen and she handed me a red pepper. I got some of the juice on my hand. The next time I tried to suck my thumb, wham! That pretty much stopped me from sucking my thumb again."

Miss Bessie cleared her throat. Clearly, I had broken her train of thought.

"When I was in the first grade," she continued as if my story was just an interruption, "my teacher put a nickel, a dime, and a penny on the desk and asked me to pick out the most valuable. I eyed them closely, then said, 'the big one.' Since that was the first time I'd seen money, I didn't know the value of one from the other. I learned it wasn't the size of the money that mattered. I think that applies to offerings, don't you, Preacher?"

I felt her penetrating eyes probing me. My recent sermon on tithing came to mind.

She continued, "My brother and I had to walk to school. Back then, there were no busses to carry us to school. We had to walk most everywhere. Anyway, we walked past a row of old rusty mailboxes with their flaps hanging open and it reminded me of a mess of fish.

One day, my brother asked, 'Aren't those rows of corn pretty and straight? I would love to plow like that. I had to admit they were pretty and straight, but I didn't want to be the one making them. From then on I determined I was not going to spend the rest of my life behind a plow. I'd seen how hard men had to work in the field and I didn't want any part of it."

Having grown up in the city and not on a farm, I couldn't relate. However, I knew she didn't tell me that story for the fun of it. She was making a point which I had yet to see.

She turned to face me and asked, "Is that why you went into the ministry?"

Chapter Eleven

O Christmas Tree, O Christmas Tree

It was December 24th and old man winter paid us an early visit that year as a vigorous wind blew in from the north. From my office window, I watched the pin oaks and pine trees sway gently. According to the Farmer's Almanac, we were in for a long and brutal season. I just hoped it wouldn't prove as deadly as the last one. That was the year we lost five souls of our small congregation. If we lost many more the Director of the Northwest District would close the church and assign me to another flock of believers.

Being a young pastor and unable to get a fill-in, I decided to stay in town to minister to my struggling congregation. After having visited every church member, active and inactive, I was fairly knowledgeable of the goings on in our church and the surrounding community.

There was Amon Culbertson, who'd overcharged Raymond Blackburn for a cord of wood; a move which cost him his position as chairman of the deacons. Then there was Sara Ray Dobbins Long Abercorn. Her claim to her first husband's farm after his passing caused such a ruckus, that we had to threaten her with church action. That decision divided the congregation since her second and third husbands were Mr. Dobbin's nephews.

Then there was Miss Bessie.

Her prayer chain worked better than email by a mile and a half.

My brief encounters with this dear saint were both insightful and instructive. Her pithy statements often shrouded a salient point, most of the time for my benefit.

The phone rang and since I was the pastor, secretary, maintenance man, and janitor, it fell upon me to answer it.

"Beulah Church," I answered, having dropped the name Methodist.

"Preacher," Miss Bessie's craggy voice cut through the connection. "I heard tell you were stayin' in town over Christmas. Is that about right?"

To me, it seemed more of an accusation than a question.

"Yes, ma'am," feeling like I'd just stepped into a bear trap.

"No one should be alone at Christmas," she proclaimed.

I wasn't sure if she was speaking of herself or of me.

"Yes, ma'am. I thought I'd stay and hold a candlelight service on Christmas Eve—"

"Won't work … no one would come," she said, not missing a beat.

Straightening, I leaned my elbows on the desk. "And why is that, Miss Bessie?"

"'Cause Preacher, that's family night. It's almost sacred. Country folk put a high value on family. Not like those city folk."

I felt the first jab of what I knew would be many more to come if I continued.

"I never thought about that. Maybe we should have it on Christmas Day."

"Nope. Everyone goes to visit their kinfolk."

Undeterred, I tried one more time. "How about New Year's Eve?"

"No one will come." She cut me off at the pass. "Too many drunks out on the highways. It's too dangerous."

Feeling like someone took a pin to my balloon; I slumped back in my chair. "Well then what do you suggest, Miss Bessie?"

Without taking a breath, she continued. "Why don't you come out here? I've cut down a Christmas tree and I need you to help me put it up. It'll be the first Christmas tree since Ned passed, God rest his soul."

She sure knew how to put a man on a guilt trip. Swallowing hard, I considered my options. I could either listen to Bing Crosby sing "White Christmas" and eat Christmas dinner at the Iron Skillet or enjoy a home cooked meal with a lonely saint.

I released a heavy sigh, and relented. "Okay, Miss Bessie, when do you want me to come?"

"Weather's turning, maybe you should come now. That way you won't get stuck in the mud like you did the last time you came. Farmer John is still laughing at you, covered up to your tush in mud."

There it was; jab number two. I hoped I could endure a day of them without going crazy.

The sun jabbed silver shafts of light through the curtained window, scattering the night and forcing its shadows into submission. I awoke to the clatter of pots and pans and Miss Bessie's gravelly humming. Apparently, she'd been up for quite a while. Her hair had been pulled up in a fresh bun, and it looked like she'd spent an extra minute in front of the mirror. The pink rouge and heavy eyeliner reminded me of a caricature of a clown.

"Miss Bessie, you look absolutely stunning," I lied, adding to my list of sins.

With a wave, she brushed my overly thick compliment aside. "Now Preacher, you needn't exaggerate. We get plenty of that on Sunday's too."

Zing!

"By the way, Merry Christmas."

It had totally slipped my mind that it was December 25th. "Merry Christmas. After breakfast, I thought we'd tackle that tree. With a little luck, we can get it up and dressed before I leave. "

After taking her seat, she offered me a hearty breakfast of ham, eggs, grits, and red-eye gravy over biscuits. When I finished, I leaned back and rubbed my overly stretched shirt. "Why Miss Bessie, I do believe my shirt has shrunk." I couldn't help grinning at my own goofy statement.

She smiled. "If you had a good southern wife, you'd be used to eatin' like that every mornin' instead of spending the church's money at the Iron Skillet." Suddenly, Miss Bessie's hand clapped over her mouth.

"Now, Miss Bessie, those folks down at the Iron Skillet are good tithing church members like you. So what goes around; comes around in my book."

Count one for the preacher …

Miss Bessie's cheeks pinked.

I downed one last cup of coffee, tugged on Ned's boots, and jammed my arms through the sleeves of my coat.

After hours of sawing limbs, and hacking away at the trunk, I finally dragged the monster tree through the front door. All-be-it, it had been greatly reduced in size. I stomped my numb feet as I stood in front of the fireplace and admired my work. "That tree sure looks good."

Taking her place next to me, she patted my shoulder. "Yep, but wait until you see it fully decorated. Macy's Christmas tree won't hold a candle to it." Her face beamed like a child's. I could have sworn she looked twenty years younger.

Two hours later, we stepped back and admired our work. It glittered with colored lights, tinsel, red, green and gold bulbs and a flossy white angel on top.

"Ain't she a beauty," Miss Bessie said, proudly. "All's we need now are a few gifts, under the tree." As she spoke, she disappeared around the corner.

Moments later, she reemerged bearing a large, brightly wrapped box. With care, she laid it under one of the low hanging branches, then stood, hands on her hips.

"Excuse me, Miss Bessie," I said and sprinted into the guest bedroom. The chilled air took my breath away and I hastily rooted though my things until I found my query. Returning with a triumphant smile, I gently laid the yellow and green flowered box under the tree.

"I never saw Christmas wrap like that before," she mused.

I smiled. "It's the thought that counts."

That's two for me …

With a shrug, she glanced up. "Well, Farmer Brown will be

here directly. He'll have your car hitched up in a jiffy and you'll be on your way. Let's exchange gifts now before he arrives."

Sensing her anticipation, I knelt down and pulled her gift from where I placed it. "It's not much. Actually, I'd planned on giving this to my mom, but with all that's going on at church—"

A gnarled hand patted mine. "That's all right, Son. Any gift good enough for your mother is good enough for me."

She took the proffered gift, and, in childlike manner, tore the wrapping paper off and tossed it aside. With a grand sweep, she lifted the lid and pulled out the purple sweater I'd purchased months ago.

"Why Preacher, this is the nicest gift I've ever received." Leaning forward, she placed a soft kiss on my forehead. The warmth of her lips radiated throughout my body and touched my soul. This truly is a saint of God.

Then, with care, she knelt and retrieved her gift. The value in scotch tape alone made the item worth the wait.

"This wrapping paper is almost too pretty to rip open, but here goes." With flair, and much to her delight, I tore off the colorful wrapping and opened the box. Inside, lay an old tattered Bible."

"That was Ned's," she croaked before her throat closed.

Fingering the tattered tomb, I opened its yellowed pages. It was marked with red lines, added notes and tears. "I will treasure this for the rest of my life," I said, clutching it to my heaving chest.

After a moment, Miss Bessie regained her composure. "Good, you might even try preaching from it once in a while. You'd be surprised at the results."

Zing … ouch.

Chapter Twelve

The Baptism of Miss Bessie

I knew when the phone rang who it was. After preaching on baptism, in which I offered several approaches to the command, I left the podium feeling rather good that I didn't offend anyone and yet still left the door open to opposing views. For a moment, I considered sending a written transcript of my sermon notes to headquarters with the hope of getting it published in the synod paper. However, upon reflection, I changed my mind. It would be better if the head deacon recommended it. *I'll call him later today and see if he is open to the idea.* That thought was shaken loose after the third ring.

The raggedy voice of Miss Bessy echoed through the connection with a renewed urgency. Hoping it wasn't another emergency like burying her dog or retrieving her overdue tithe, I braced myself for what I knew would be an interesting request.

"Hello to you too, Miss Bessie. How may I serve you, today?" I rebuked myself for sounding so piously humble, but she had a way of eliciting such words before I could stop them.

"Preacher, I need to be baptized, and I mean in the river."

My mind stumbled at the sudden and strange request. I had assumed that matter had been taken care of long before I was born. Sputtering, I tried to keep my voice level, although my mind scrambled. "But Miss Bessie, I thought—"

"Nope, you thought wrong, Preacher. Ned was, but not me. You see, I'm afraid of water."

Her statement struck me as odd. I had assumed the leathery old saint feared neither God nor man.

"Never liked to go swimming or even be in a boat," she continued. "I hate to be splashed in the face so forget sprinkling. The notion of being dipped frightens me to death, but after your sermon . . . well." She let her voice trail off.

My sermon? I thought. I didn't actually try to convince anyone to be baptized. That was the weekly message and I dutifully preached it, albeit, not with a lot of conviction.

"It was in the summer of 1942," I heard her saying. "Reverend Grizzard came storming into town preaching hellfire, got everyone upset. Momma and us kids loaded up the two mule wagon and went to the revival, us and as many people as we could fit in. Daddy had nothing to do with going.

Reverend Grizzard preached on John 3:16 every night. This went on for quite some time. When he finished each night he'd say, 'turn loose and come down the aisle.'

I looked down, and my knuckles were white from holding onto the pew. But I turned loose and walked down the aisle. I got down front, knelt on the old-fashioned kneeling bench, and asked God to forgive my sins.

I told everyone in the wagon what had happened and they thought I was talking about joining the church. But in my heart, I knew I got saved.

Before that, I thought I had about a 70% chance of going to Heaven. But I knew how ornery I was. I also thought I had to be baptized to get saved and I was scared to death of water."

"Miss Bessie, you know the creek is frozen over. Couldn't this wait until spring? And then there is the matter of your age. I'm sure the good Lord understands. We wouldn't want you to catch pneumonia, now would we?"

Undeterred, Miss Bessie pressed on. "Now Preacher, don't stretch God's grace or underestimate my resolve in the matter. Spring is still months away and the Lord is comin''. Furthermore, I ain't getting any younger. My departure is as uncertain as the weather."

Taking a hard swallow, I shoved my reservations to a dark corner from whence they came. I too had a fear of water. Having grown up in the Midwest, I seldom saw water more than ankle deep. The few ponds that did exist were broiling with cottonmouths and I avoided them at all costs. "Well, when would you like to be baptized?"

"How about this Sunday afternoon?" She shot back without hesitation.

She left me little wiggle room. Feeling backed into a corner, I braced myself for what I knew would be a first for both of us. "All right, I'll make the arrangements. See you Sunday."

I knew praying for an ice storm would only make matters worse, so I called Jed Combie, the head deacon. Maybe he could talk some sense into her.

After one ring, the phone was picked up and Jed's booming voice resonated in my ear. "Hello?"

"Hello, Jed?—"

"I know Pastor. If you're calling about Miss Bessie, she already called me. Looks like you have a taker," he said with a dry chuckle.

Leaning back in my cushioned chair, I imagined him sitting by the hearth in front of a raging fire. "Yeah, I suppose so. Could you have a bonfire ready? She's going to be chilled to the bone when she comes out of that creek."

"I can do that, and I'll have a stack of blankets ready too. Forecasters are threatening foul weather and I'm guessing we'll all appreciate having something warm to snuggle up in."

The call ended and I reviewed my notes from Sunday's message. There it was, clear as the ears on a monkey. "Now, as they came to a body of water, the eunuch said, 'See, here is water. What hinders me from being baptized?' Philip said, 'If you believe with all your heart, you may.' The eunuch said, "I believe that Jesus Christ is the Son of God.' So he commanded the chariot to stand still. And both Philip and the eunuch went down into the water, and he baptized him."

No getting around it. Looks like I'd better start practicing.

Sunday rolled around with its usual regularity. Having practiced immersing my mop in the bathtub, I felt no more prepared to perform this rite than I did for my first dedication service. Glancing over the congregation, I caught a glimpse of Miss Bessie. There she sat, dressed in her finest. I hoped she'd have backed out, but not Miss Bessie. She wouldn't back down in an argument with the devil himself, and probably spit in his eye when she got the better of him.

At least the message I preached today was not one to provoke any major decisions . . . I hoped.

It was obvious by the attendance; word had gotten around. Every seat in our small sanctuary was filled, and the ushers had to put out the folding chairs, something they hadn't done since we churched Sara Ray Dobbins Long Abercorn.

Following the message, I dismissed the service and we filed out through the back door. Like a procession of monks, the congregation pulled their hoods over their heads and hunkered along the narrow path leading from the church building through the woods. By then, Bro. Jed Combie had started a blazing fire, and we gathered around it and waited. Glancing skyward, I noticed the pregnant clouds pressing down upon us. Within minutes, they began to release their burden, and it didn't take long before a new layer of heavy, wet flakes covered our shoulders like a bad case of dandruff. While we waited, Jimmy-Lee the only teenager lobbed a few rocks into the creek, cracking the ice and leaving a gaping hole. Ice-blue waters swirled like a washing machine. *This will give new meaning to being baptized for the remission of your sin.*

Having never baptized anyone, at least by immersion, I didn't own a pair of waders and didn't have time to buy them. So it was with much trepidation, I stepped into the icy waters. A moment later, fiery shards of pain shot up my legs. Instinctively, I sucked in a sharp breath much to the amusement of my flock. *This must have been how it felt for the passengers of the Titanic.* As the numbing waters gathered around my waist, I wondered if my hands would function long enough to place this dear saint under the water and lift her up. I also wondered if the shock would stop her heart halfway through the process. *Lordy, Lordy! Help us.*

As I waited, teeth chattering, the crowd parted and Miss Bessie stood in the gap robed in white. My heart sank. I had hoped she'd chicken out or at least come dressed in something warmer. Then again, if she did, she would soon be soaked in frozen water and it would take even longer to warm her up. Clever gal, I mused.

Taking a shaky breath, she stepped into the swirling waters. By now, I had no feeling in my legs. I could tell by the look on her face, she felt the same spikes of pain as I did when I first entered the waters. I wondered if she now regretted her decision . . . I did.

"Go ahead, Preacher. Let's get on with it before we both freeze to death," she stuttered through chattering teeth.

Needing no prodding, I began the ritual. "Miss Bessie, do you believe in Jesus?"

Eyes closed, a radiant smile stretched across her face. "Yes." Her voice carried across the waters clear and strong, but I knew it wouldn't last. Already, her slender frame had begun to shake. It would only be a matter of minutes and we both would be like popsicles.

Gathering my strength, I continued, "Upon your profession of faith, I baptize you my sister in the name of the Father, the Son, and the Holy Ghost."

Lifting my numb fingers, I placed them over her mouth and

eased her back. Suddenly, her eyes popped open. Her free hand grabbed my lapel and held on for dear life. As her weight tugged me forward, my unfeeling legs lost their footing and I toppled over. A rush of numbing pain stung my exposed flesh and I fought to keep from sucking in a watery breath. Like a wild bobcat, Miss Bessie's hands flailed, her legs kicked, scratching and clawing at me as if I were her executioner rather than her pastor. Then again, maybe I was.

A moment later, strong hands grabbed me by the arms and tugged us both out of the creek like two floundering pickerel. Eyes wide and gasping for air, Miss Bessie swiped the chilled water from her eyes. A bright smile lit her face. Teeth chattering, she smiled. "Did you finish?"

Her question took a moment to register my frozen brain. "Finish? Finish what?"

"You know, the saying," she sputtered.

I blinked absent-mindedly. For the life of me, I couldn't think of how the rest of the ritual went. By now, the laughing congregation had subsided and they had pulled us closer to the fire where a warm blanket and a hot cup of coffee awaited us. After a few swigs of the wicked brew, my mind thawed enough for me to remember how the rest of the baptismal service went.

Lifting my mug, I said, "Raised in the newness of life."

Miss Bessie held her mug up and tapped mine. An impish twinkle danced in her eyes. I wondered what lay behind them. It didn't take long for me to find out.

Cocking her head heavenward, she winked. "Looks like we both got baptized good and proper, Preacher. I think the Lord is pleased. Don't you?"

It suddenly dawned on me. I had never been scripturally baptized, at least not until now. Nodding, I returned her shivering smile. "Yes, ma'am. I believe He's pleased . . . with both of us."

Chapter Thirteen

The Passing of Ole Blue

It was another gray day in February. The steel clouds hung low blanketing our corner of the world like a bad mood. I'd labored all week trying to come up with a sermon that would lift the spirits of my beleaguered congregation, but it was hard to do when I, myself was in the doldrums. Checking the liturgical calendar for ideas, I found the, usually boring, *suggested sermon* of the week. My stomach flipped. *Sorry Lord, but I just can't bring myself to preach another message from First John.*

With Ground Hog day just around the corner, I found little to sink my teeth into. Not that I'd ever consider eating one of those varmints, but I was getting desperate. Sunday loomed over me like those gray clouds blocking out any sunlight, any ray of hope, any word from God.

I was about to call it a day and head out to the Iron Skillet for an early supper when the phone rang. Being the only one to answer it left me in a dilemma. What if it were the head deacon? He'd wonder where I was and probably question me on Sunday. What if it was Sara Ray Dobbins Long Abercorn . . . Again? She promised to make my life miserable for kicking her out of the church and so far, she was as good as her word. I shuttered at the thought of another lengthy conversation with her. Conversation, I huffed. More like a diatribe.

As the insistent ringing drilled into my psyche, calling me back to reality, my conscience suddenly awakened. *What if it was someone in real need?* Guilt stabbed me and I snatched the phone from its cradle.

"Beulah Church, this is Pastor—"

"Preacher," the gravelly voice of Miss Bessie grabbed my attention. *Had she been crying?* I'd never known this leathery old saint to cry. She was rock solid in her faith. Even more so than me, especially when it came to the sovereignty of God and the peculiar goings-on of man.

"Yes, Miss Bessie?" I uttered.

"Preacher, he's gone." Her voice broke, and my heart shuddered. I hated it when women cried over the phone. I was helpless to do much, and words always seemed to get in the way of real comfort.

"Who, Miss Bessie? Who's gone?"

She took a long, halting breath and spoke. Her throat closed, keeping her from speaking more than a whisper. "Ole' Blue. He died last night."

The image of the old blue-tick hound with his tongue hanging out the side of his mouth as he loped across the yard came to mind. Conscience and my better-self stifled the urge to laugh. I was surprised the old coot hadn't died years ago or had been shot by Miss Bessie herself after what he'd done to her the night he cold-nosed her in the chicken coop.

"I'm so sorry to hear that, Miss Bessie," I lied. "Is there anything I can do?" No sooner had the words escaped my mouth than I regretted it.

Miss Bessie cleared her throat. "Yes, could you come out and bury him? He was such a good dog." Her voice cracked and I heard her muffled cry.

I swallowed the lump in my throat. Although I had no love loss for the old mutt, I cared for Miss Bessie. It was Miss Bessie, who'd cast the deciding vote to accept me as the church's latest pastor. Although rumor had it, she was also the one who cast the deciding vote to oust the last pastor.

"Why, yes, Miss Bessie, I'd be honored." My smooth tone sounded more like a funeral home director than a preacher from the hill country. It took days for my throat and voice to return to normal after the Sunday sermon. The louder the better. That's how they liked it, as proven by the rhythmic cadence coming from the, "amen corner."

Shoving my notes aside, I stood. "When would you like me to come?" I knew what she'd say before she said it.

"Can you come directly?"

"Yes, ma'am, I just need to run by my house and change clothes."

"No need to do that, Preacher. I've already dug the hole. I just need you to say a few words before we commit him to God's care."

Again, the urge to laugh percolated in my chest, but I managed to quash it. "Yes, ma'am. I'll be right out." My tone sounded as pious as the pope, but what else could I say?

Forty-five minutes later, my car ground to a halt in front of Miss Bessie's home. Nothing had changed since the last time I'd been there. As a matter of fact, except for not seeing Ole Blue lounging on the porch, not much had changed since the first time I'd visited her.

Getting out of my car, I made my way to the porch. The first step creaked as I placed my weight upon it. "The door's open, Preacher. Come on in and set a spell. I'll just be a minute."

She sounded better, more in control of her emotions.

"Yes, ma'am." I knew not to question her. She had her own way of doing things.

As I reclined on the couch, a peace settled over me. In the background, the ticking of a Regulator clock beat out a steady rhythm. The crackle of a fire in the hearth warmed me and I felt at home. I inhaled catching a familiar aroma. Was that roast beef I smelled? As I listened, I heard the low boil of something cooking on the wood-burning stove. Was this the real reason she'd called for me? And why hadn't she called Farmer Brown to come out and do the honor?

Movement flickered at the edges of my mind and I turned. Miss Bessie steadied herself against the door frame. Her slender form shrouded in black. She lifted the black veil which hung from a black, flossy hat and gave me a weak smile. "It's only fittin' we give Ole Blue a proper burial, isn't it?"

I nodded. Wished I'd had a comforting word . . . none came to mind.

Offering me her elbow, she continued. "Did you bring Ned's Bible?"

Padding the old tomb sitting next to me, I smiled. "Yes, ma'am. I thought you might ask."

She bent her head with a slight tilt. "You're learnin', Preacher. Now let's go. The sun is settin' and I don't want the day to end before we've said our good-byes."

There were still six hours left in the day but to tell her that felt somewhat useless. As far as Miss Bessie was concerned, the day ended at sundown and that was that.

Together, we took a slow and steady pace through the kitchen and out the back door. We made our way past the garden, now covered with leaves, and found a lonely plot of land near the tree line. A rusting shovel stood silent vigil over a newly dug grave, its ancient blade jammed deep into the soil. Clods of earth lay aside a small wooden box, while two chairs waited for the only mourners of a lifelong companion. An old board with the hastily painted words, 'Here Lies Ole' Blue, My Best Friend,' rested against an oak tree. Its barren limbs, stripped of all but the most tenacious leaves clawed the vacant sky.

Tears splashed down my cheeks unhindered and I envied this dear woman. I didn't have a close friend, let alone a dog. I determined that moment to get one . . . a dog that is. A friend? That was a different story. Maybe Miss Bessie could be my friend . . . I prayed so.

Miss Bessie's ragged voice broke my musings. "Preacher, do you believe dogs go to Heaven?"

The thought had never occurred to me. I knew the Bible spoke of dogs, mostly in a derogatory way. There was the passage about the little dogs that ate the crumbs which fell from the master's table. And there were the dogs that ministered to old Lazarus, so maybe it evened out in the long-run.

"Yes, Miss Bessie, I think most dogs go to Heaven, at least the good ones," I said, trying to sound confident, which I wasn't.

I steadied the dear saint as she placed the box in the ground and took her seat.

"Preacher, would you kindly say a few words before we close the grave?

I nodded, stood and cleared my throat. Having Googled Chaplin's Prayers from the Common Book of Prayers, I felt better prepared than on most Sundays. Opening the tattered Bible, I found the notes I'd scribbled.

Rocking back on my heels, I began in my most somber tone. "Give rest, O Christ, to thy, uh, to thy servant's friend, where sorrow and pain are no more, neither sighing, but life everlasting. Into thy hands, O merciful Savior, we commend our friend. Acknowledge, we humbly beseech thee, a sheep of thine own fold, a lamb of thine own flock and receive him into the arms of mercy, into the blessed rest of everlasting peace. And wait for the general resurrection where we shall all live together in thy glorious kingdom. Amen."

I slowly closed my Bible and took a seat next to Miss Bessie. A solo tear coursed down her wrinkled cheek and she sniffed. Reaching out, I took her gnarled hand and gave it a gentle squeeze.

She returned it and spoke softly. "You know Preacher; I was wrong about one thing." Her steady gaze locked on mine.

"What's that, Miss Bessie?"

She stood and smoothed out her skirt. "I said Ole' Blue was my best friend, but I was wrong. You are."

Chapter Fourteen

Miss Bessie on the Subject of Courting

It was the first nice spring day in weeks and I was determined to take full advantage of it. I had my eye on Iris Ashcroft, the Baptist minister's daughter ever since Time Change Sunday. Maybe Daylight Savings Time gave me a new outlook on life and its meaning. Yes, I settled the spiritual matters and yes, I was on my way to sanctification ... or so I hoped. I'm sure Miss Bessie would be quick to differ with my assessment, but she was not here.

No ... today, I was free ... free to feel, to breathe, to pursue love. I silently thanked my high school English Literature teacher, Mrs. Wellington, for forcing me to memorize Alfred Lord Tennyson's *Locksley Hall.* The lines of which I hoped would take on new meaning ... 'In the Spring a livelier iris changes on the burnish'd dove; In the Spring a young man's fancy lightly turns to thoughts of love.'

I spent the entire afternoon with Iris Ashcroft sitting on a grassy knoll overlooking Lake Chehaw, a reservoir built to collect the waters of the Flint River, the Kinchafoonee Creek, and

Muckalee Creek. Not far from our perch was the Flint Dam, built in 1908 as the hydroelectric generation was just getting to Georgia. It did not escape my notice that her name echoed through the aforementioned poem. I smiled at the thought.

It was not only the perfect setting for my first romantic venture, but it was a perfect way to get to know Miss Iris. Her father insisted I maintain the formality until we received his permission to be on a first name basis. I kinda liked it, however ... it gave the setting a playful atmosphere.

In the distance, we listened to motorboats and jet skis skittering across the blue water. Graceful sailboats moved silently with the steady breeze and I imagined myself on one. As we ate our lunch I smiled as one such boat caught a gust of wind and tipped over, throwing its skipper and only passenger overboard. Their laughter echoed across the waves, up the shore and brought smiles to our faces. I loved to see Iris smile, hear her laughter, catch the twinkle in her eyes. Yes, this was a good day ... to fall in love.

Our conversation bounced from politics to religion and came full circle to our respective families. Mine was pretty simple ... I was an only child, an overachiever, not into sports, but very much into books and movies. Iris, on the other hand, had no trouble divulging her family history. Maybe it was the chocolate cake she'd made from scratch, but I got the distinct impression she felt the same intoxicating effects of an extra shot of espresso she'd added. I certainly felt it. Once she started, it was tricky to get her to take a breath. Her animated descriptions of her cousins and uncles left me grasping for something solid. By the time she'd finished, my head swirled with anecdotal facts, which I hoped I'd not be required to repeat.

It didn't seem that long, but by the time we'd finished eating, talking, and laughing, the sun bid us a fond farewell to today's pleasantries. Long shadows from a nearby tree line, like fingers, clawed across the meadow. The breeze freshened and Iris rubbed her hands over her bare arms to chase the 'shiver-flesh,' as she called it. Our picnic ended all too soon. I made a mental note to plan another one as soon as my schedule allowed.

Standing up, I extended my hand and helped Iris to her feet. She stood and straightened out her yellow sun-dress, then gave me one of those to-the-moon smiles. My heart missed a cog and I wondered if she too felt the same light-headedness. Being careful not to let my feelings get the better of me, I resisted the urge to take her in my arms. Rather, I turned my attention to cleaning up. As I lifted one corner of the blanket, Iris grabbed the other corner and shook it sending crumbs and grass in the air. Laughing wildly, she swatted a grass clipping from my face. I felt heat creep up my neck and hoped she didn't see my befuddlement.

After placing the remnants of lunch in the picnic basket ... a four inch Italian sub, a bag of chips, a half bottle of the sweetest tea money could buy (from the Golden Arches), and three-quarters of the best chocolate cake I'd ever eaten, I carried it to my car and waited for Iris to finish folding the blanket.

The trip from the lake to Iris's house took all of twenty minutes; minutes I would cherish until the next time we were together. After walking her to the front door of the parsonage ... a two-story white Colonial, I held out my hand expecting the cursory handshake. To my surprise and ecstatic delight, she stood on her tiptoes and gave me a quick peck on the cheek. With a light chuckle, she scampered inside the house before her doting father had a chance to swing the door open.

I floated to my car ... turned the key. The battery sent a surge of electricity into the already running generator jolting me back to reality. A quick glance at the house ... relief ... she wasn't looking ... probably preoccupied with telling her parents about her afternoon.

As I returned to my one-room apartment over the Newberry's garage, I noticed a tattered pickup truck sitting on the shoulder of the road. A set of overall-covered legs protruded from under the engine compartment kicking like the upper half of their owner had tangled with a bobcat.

It was Buford, Miss Bessie's nephew. I pulled to the shoulder of the road and got out. "Need a hand?" I asked, knowing my only aid might be to give Buford a tool if needed.

A large, oil-blackened hand extended from under the wheel-well. "Hand me that big hammah."

I stepped to the rear of the truck and gazed into a large toolbox. Inside, an assortment of wrenches, screwdrivers, and tools lay in neat rows. It took me only a minute to find a rather large "sledgehammah." Hoping it was what Buford wanted; I returned and placed the handle in the palm of his waiting hand. I felt somewhat like a surgeon's assistant.

"Yep, that's the one. Thanks, Reverend."

As the hammering began, I wondered how he knew it was me. Maybe it was my shoes. After three or four whacks, Buford gave a satisfied grunt.

"Say Rev … could you crank the engine? That would save me the trouble from having to crawl out from under thishere thang."

Knowing what he meant by 'crank the engine,' I climbed behind the grubby steering wheel and started to pump the gas when—"don't touch the gas pedal—just turn the key."

My foot froze.

I turned the key.

Chug, chug, belch.

A large puff of black smoke escaped the muffler followed by Buford turning the air purple with an oath that would make most sailors blush.

"Sorry, Rev, I forgot it was you. Sit tight while I make a few more adjustments." The hammering resumed.

It was then, I noticed Miss Bessie. She was sitting on a lawn chair in the shade ... hands folded ... a pert smile tickled the corners of the mouth. She stood, folded the chair and got in the passenger side.

"Preacher," she said with a slight nod. "Did'ya enjoy your date with Miss Iris?"

I felt my eyes widen. How did she know about my *date?* My personal life was a closely guarded secret. If she knew, then so did everyone up and down the prayer chain. I'd be inundated the following Sunday with questions about my love life. Knowing it was useless to deny her observation; I smiled and let out a breath.

"Yes, Miss Bessie, we had a wonderful time. Can we talk about something else?"

"Did the Reverend Ashcroft insist you call his daughter, Miss Iris?" her eyes twinkled with an impish gleam.

She'd make a great lawyer—"Yes ... how'd you know?" I regretted the question the moment I asked it.

"'cause Preacher, he makes all her suitors call her that."

I was hooked … other suitors? How many had there been before me? I resisted the urge to ask, knowing Miss Bessie probably knew the answer.

"Anyway, you can't keep a secret for long in this small town."

"Yes, ma'am. What's wrong with Buford's truck?"

"Did she kiss you?"

My heart sank to the floorboard. I had to fight the urge to keep from hitting the gas pedal.

"Miss Bessie, with all due respect, I plead the fifth."

"That's okay. Your secret's safe with me."

I wasn't so sure.

"But if you ask me, I think she's the right one." She left the statement hang like a slow curve-ball.

I couldn't help myself—"How can you say such a thing?"

Miss Bessie's face beamed. "I've seen the way she looks at you …"

My head swirled. "When did you see Miss Iris looking at me?" I couldn't believe I was having this conversation … not with Miss Bessie … not with anyone.

Placing a finger to her pinkish cheek, she fained reflection. "Let's see … there was the time she sang at Tommy Wolford's funeral. Her face lit up like a child getting their first silver dollar. And then there was the citywide Fourth of July picnic. She sang the national anthem like a bird. But when you gave the invocation, she couldn't take her eyes off of you."

I shifted to look Miss Bessie directly in the face. "Now how do you know that?"

Fanning herself, Miss Bessie's slight shoulders rose and fell— "I peeked ... but only a second," she hastened to say. "She looked almost angelic."

"You saw all that in just a peek?"

"Well—maybe it was more like a glance rather than a peek, but—"

I nodded. "So what should I do? I've only been with her once, and her father, the Reverend Ashcroft, insisted we follow a prescribed series of steps called, 'Courtship.'"

Miss Bessie folded her hands on her lap. "Yes, that's what it's called. Back in my day, that's how it was done. You win the father's heart before you win his daughter's."

Hands held in surrender, I was incredulous. "I'm not marrying her father, I'm—"

I'd blown it. How did she get me talking about marrying Iris? We'd dated once and now Miss Bessie had me talking marriage?

"Look, Miss Bessie, this conversation is over. My romantic life is not open to discussion, especially not with—" I bit my tongue.

"If you ask her, she'll say yes," came Buford's gruff voice.

My head whipped around. I was outmaneuvered, and I knew it.

"Your truck wasn't broken down was it Buford?" The burly nephew stood with one arm draped inside the driver side window, the other hanging on the mirror.

He offered me a crooked grin. "Nope, it was Miss Bessie's idea." Then he spat a glob of brown juice and wiped his mouth with the back of his greasy hand. "But she's right ... she always is."

I cut my eyes in Miss Bessie's direction. "I don't suppose you've already talked with the good reverend?"

"Well, let's just say, 'God works in mysterious ways, His wonders to perform.'"

Chapter Fifteen

Marriage and Miss Bessie

After having been duped into stopping to help Buford, my mood had changed for the worse. All memory of my delightful day with Iris was gone. Getting out of his truck, I headed back to my car, my shoulders slumping.

"Mind if I tag along? Buford's going the other direction and it's too far for me to walk." I knew to say no was not an option.

"Okay," I said with resignation. She had more to say, of that I was sure.

She slid in, clicked her seat belt and smiled. "Have I told you about the time Ned proposed to me?"

Feeling trapped, I started the engine. It was going to be a long trip. "No, Miss Bessie. Tell me about it," my voice belied my inner thoughts.

"Well, it wasn't much as far as proposals go. We'd been courting for some time and one day, out of the blue, he said, 'When are we going to get married?' I have to admit, I was taken aback. We were sitting on the front porch of my parents' house and

I had one of those fans, you know ... the kind you get at the funeral parlor? I fanned myself to keep from passing out.

'As soon as school lets out, I guess,' I said, my voice barely above a whisper.

At the time, I was just sixteen and a half. Back then, high school went through eleventh grade. Neither of us knew what we were doing, but it was common in those days. When a girl graduated from high school, she got married.

In May of that year, Ned went to the courthouse and filled out the paperwork for our marriage license. Then he posted it on the public notice board. Back then, if you couldn't get your parent's approval, you posted the announcement on the bulletin board down at the courthouse for a week. If nobody takes it down, you could get married. So he put it posted it and we waited. It was the longest week of my life. I didn't tell anyone about it. Since daddy didn't go to town, but once or twice a year, I knew he'd never see it.

Later that week, Ned stopped by the house and asked daddy if he could marry me.

I watched from inside the house nearly biting my thumbnail to a nub as the two men talked. Later, Ned told me my dad asked what he'd do if he said no."

"What did he say," I blurted without thinking.

Miss Bessie chuckled. "Ned told him that he'd posted the

license down at the courthouse a week ago. 'Well, I don't guess I've got anything to say about it, now do I?' Then he turned and walked slowly up the steps into the house.

When he told me what my daddy said, I didn't know if I should laugh or cry. I felt bad that we'd deceived my daddy. Now, I'm not saying that's how it should be done, and I'm sure if he could have it to do over, Ned would have done it differently, but it was too late. Later, Ned apologized and daddy and momma got settled with the idea.

We wanted to get married on June 4th, which was on a Saturday. But the problem was, we didn't have a car. So word got around and my uncle, you know, the one with the Edsel, picked us up and drove us to the Office of the Justice of the Peace.

With it being Saturday, the office was closed, so we headed to his house, hoping he was home. We rumbled up to his house just as he was coming out with a bucket of slop to feed the hogs.

My uncle eased the car to a stop, got out and said, 'Sir, I've got a couple of kids in the back seat who want to get married.'

He laughed, set the bucket down and leaned in. 'Do you have your license?'

Ned had borrowed a white woolen suit for the occasion, and was sweating like a glass of tea on a summer day. He looked at me and asked, 'Did you remember to bring it?'

I took a dry swallow and handed him the folded envelope. The Justice scanned it, then climbed in the front seat. I laugh every time I think about it now, but back then, we were as nervous as two long-tailed cats in a room full of rocking chairs.

It was three o'clock and the sun was beating down on the top of that black Edsel like a torch. It was all I could do to keep from passing out.

Finally, the Justice let out a slow breath and said, 'Well, everything looks in order. Let's get on with it.'

After mopping his brow with a handkerchief, he pulled a little book from his back pocket and began to read the wedding vows. When he came to the part where you say, 'I will,' I was so scared, my mouth felt like I'd swallowed a persimmon. I croaked out a dry, 'I will.'

Then it was Ned's turn to speak. His voice rang out as clear as a Pentecostal preacher on Sunday at noon. 'I will,' he said.

The Justice peered at us over his bifocals and said, 'Okay, you're married. Now go and have fun.'"

By the time she finished her story, we'd arrived at her home and I parked under the large shade tree occupying the center of her yard. We sat there for a minute savoring the moment when Miss Bessie broke the silence.

"That day, Ned promised me one thing. He said, there was one word we'd never use in our home." She paused as if on cue.

"What word was that? I heard myself asking."

She turned to face me. Her jaw set, her eyes burned like two embers. "Now Preacher, I know it's not popular today, what with the church taking a weaker position on marriage, but he said, 'we would never say the word, divorce in our home, as long as we lived.'"

I was both encouraged and smitten with guilt as it was recently announced that our denomination had softened its stance on the permanence of marriage.

"You know Miss Bessie, if it's good enough for you and Ned; it's good enough for me."

With that, she smiled and got out. "So when are you two tying the knot?"

"Miss Bessie—!"

Chapter Sixteen

Miss Bessie on the Topic of Marriage

It has been said, 'News of my demise has been greatly exaggerated.' Well, news of my engagement had been greatly exaggerated. Such was the case with me and Miss Iris. I actually had not proposed and she had actually not accepted, but according to Miss Bessie, it was a done deal.

Our courtship lasted all of six months and already the prayer chain/grapevine buzzed with stories of an alleged torrid affair. Although I don't know how torrid anything could be having to double-date with one's own future In-law.

Nevertheless, it was my plan to ask Reverend Ashcroft for his daughter, Iris' hand in marriage and I was fairly confident he would agree. Thus, it was a trick to keep my plan to propose a secret until I asked her without Miss Bessie catching wind of it and tipping her off.

So, when the phone in my office rang, I instinctively knew who it was. After checking the caller ID, I smiled grimly. If there was one thing I'd learned from Miss Bessie, it was persistence. She was the most persistent person I knew when it came to getting something she wanted.

Whether it was spiritual or not, she was relentless. It seemed, even when she prayed, she shook the heavens until God himself yielded to her demands. And when it came to other matters … woe be to the person who stood between Miss Bessie and her goal. Today was no exception. As I glanced at the clock, I had to smile … right on time.

"Preacher?" she asked in her usual crotchety voice. "I don't suppose you've popped the question yet." It was as much a question as it was an indictment.

"No, Miss Bessie, not since yesterday."

"You are planning on asking her, aren't you?" she fired back.

"Yes, ma'am, but I'm waiting for the right time."

"And that would be—"

We've had this conversation before. Her continued probes felt more like an interrogation rather than a quest for information.

"You know Preacher, time is not on your side. There are other suitors interested in Miss Iris."

I knew where she was going with this. "If you're referring to your nephew, Buford, I don't think I have much to worry about."

"Nope."

Her one-word response sent a chill down my back. In a town as small as ours, finding a single, male suitor of the caliber necessary to meet Reverend Ashcroft's standards was a challenge at best. Knowing I had a rival in the field of courtship made me do some quick reconnoitering.

"Oh? Who might that be?" My mind raced through the short list of possible candidates.

"His name is William Oliver Norstrum III. He's the Baptist Association's president's son."

My heart dropped like a pebble down a deep well. I could see the odds stacking up against me. After all, I was just the pastor of a small, independent Methodist Church and William Oliver Norstrum III had a pedigree a mile long. I felt like a nag in a race against thoroughbreds.

"So what are my chances?" I asked, more out of inner thought than seeking advice.

"Not good Preacher. You need to strike while the iron is hot."

"Miss Bessie, you're not suggesting Miss Iris likes Mr. William Oliver Norstrum III better than me, are you?"

"No, but I am saying the Reverend Ashcroft likes the sound of Iris Norstrum, better than Iris Wallace."

Her statement hit me like a bale of hay, I had to admit. I'd taken my relationship with Iris for granted. I had moved at my usual unhurried pace. My heart rate quickened as I saw my opportunity slipping away. "What do you suggest, Miss Bessie?"

My lack of skill in the romantic department was more than obvious. I needed some wise counsel and I was sure Miss Bessie was quite ready to offer me as much as I wanted.

"Take my advice: plan a nice dinner at an expensive restaurant. Buy her a dozen roses. Have a musician walk around playing the violin. That should do it."

It suddenly dawned on me. I was the one being played like a violin. If I took her advice, not only would my church and half the town know about it, but so would Iris.

"Miss Bessie," I said, "just how close is Mr. William Oliver Norstrum III to asking for Iris's hand in marriage?"

"Uh, well, actually…"

"That's what I thought. Is there actually a William Oliver Norstrum III?"

"Yes," her voice wobbled and I knew I'd hit pay dirt.

"And just how old is William Oliver Norstrum III?"

"Uh … seven? But she really does love him." She quickly added.

"I'm sure she does, Miss Bessie, I'm sure she does. Are there any more gems of wisdom you have to impart?"

After a thoughtful pause she spoke, but this time, it was with less confidence. "Preacher, I have lived and I have loved, and I have been loved. Now those days are a quiet memory. If I had it to do over, I'd do it in a heartbeat. And I'd do it sooner rather than later. So my advice to you is this: ask Iris to marry you and do it soon. Then tell her you love her every day you live." Her voice broke and if I could, I was sure I would have seen a silver tear caressing her rosy cheek.

She took a shaky breath and continued. "Preacher, it's been a long time since I've heard someone say, 'I love you.'"

That was it … my heart shattered. From that moment, I knew what I had to do. I would ask Miss Iris to marry me the next time I saw her, but first I had something to say to Miss Bessie. I took a hard swallow, then cleared my throat. "Thank you, Miss Bessie … I love you."

Chapter Seventeen

The Elixir of Love

The day started most unexpectedly.

After months of planning, my wedding day finally arrived … along with the worst case of laryngitis I ever experienced. I've had throat trouble in the past. It's one of the hazards of being a preacher in this part of the country. But the timing couldn't have been worse.

Knowing my bride-to-be expected a resounding "I do" to the questions about "Do you take this woman …," I didn't want to disappoint her, the officiating preacher, Iris's parents, and my church congregation.

Desperate to regain the use of my voice, I tried humming.

Nothing!

Nada, zilch!

I tried gargling with warm salt water, hoping it would help … it didn't.

Neither did honey and vinegar nor did a warm wet towel wrapped around my throat, except to make me look silly.

Calling for help was about as useful as calling for a unanimous decision from my Deacon Board. Using sign language was also out of the question. The only sign language I knew was, "I love Jesus." Plus, it dawned on me; I didn't know anyone to translate my sign language.

With only a few hours until I was expected at the church, I saw my options thinning. Using a whiteboard to write my answers was out of the question … so was nodding or smiling or hand signs. I needed to speak, and that wasn't happening.

My phone rang.

Of all the times to get a call from Publisher's Clearinghouse telling me I'd won a million dollars.

It rang insistently.

Five rings.

Ten rings.

It's not going to quit.

It had to be Miss Bessie. No one was as persistent as her. I lifted the phone to my ear and grunted.

"Preacher?" I was right. It was her favorite way of addressing me.

"Yes?" I said in a breathy voice. No vocal folds were used in the making of that sound.

"I figured as much."

It was as if she knew and I wondered if she was prescient ... she had to be. How else could she know to call? She continued, "The way you carried on last Sunday with all that spittin' and hollerin', I knew it would catch up to ya."

I grunted.

"Don't try to speak, Preacher. It will only make matters worse."

I knew that.

"I'll be there in twenty minutes," she ended the call.

I knew it would take thirty. I also knew her nephew drove like Jehu ... wildly.

I replaced the phone to its cradle ... and prayed.

Fifteen minutes later, a heavy hand pounded on my front door.

It belonged to Buford ... Miss Bessie's corn-fed nephew.

I opened the door and was immediately thrust aside as he bulled his way past ... not speaking. I guessed Miss Bessie interrupted his nap.

Behind him, the demure frame of Miss Bessie.

Turning, I saw him flop into my favorite chair. I cringed. How did he know that was my favorite chair? Was he prescient too? I mused.

He offered me a crooked, gap-toothed smile.

"You remember my nephew, Buford, don't you?" Miss Bessie

asked.

I nodded. She and Buford had conspired to get me to meet the woman I was about to marry. That's if I could utter an ascent to the posed questions. If not, I guess I'd have to settle for a life of celibacy and poverty.

Definitely poverty.

"Well, let's get started," Miss Bessie said without preamble.

I wondered what we were about to start.

She headed to the kitchen carrying a large black bag.

Buford grinned.

My heart stuttered.

After a few minutes of banging around, Miss Bessie emerged bearing a mug. "Watch it, it's hot," she said, handing me the mug of steaming liquid.

It warmed my hands and I inhaled. There was something bitter in the aroma, but before I could raise an eyebrow, she nudged the cup closer to my lips.

Miss Bessie explained, "Now Preacher, I know you have a bit of a conviction against drinking alcohol and all, but didn't the Apostle Paul tell young Timothy to drink a little wine for his stomach ache?"

Stomach's sake ... sake ... not ache.

All at once, two burly arms belonging to Buford hugged me

from behind.

It suddenly dawned on me why she brought her nephew along.

"Open." She smiled. It wasn't a suggestion.

Miss Bessie pinched my nose.

I opened.

She tipped the mug and poured the liquid down my throat.

I coughed and sputtered as the fiery brew spread throughout my body.

She smiled.

"There now, that wasn't so bad, now was it?"

I continued to sputter.

"Give it a few minutes. If it doesn't work, we'll give you another shot."

I wondered how many shots it would take before I was completely inebriated.

Probably two … two too many.

I was right.

Feeling slightly lightheaded, I sagged into my favorite chair before Buford could repossess it and flopped down. Laying my head back, I felt the room shift. It was obvious Miss Bessie's elixir was working, but not just on my throat.

"How's the throat?" Buford asked.

I'd wondered if he suffered from the same malady. It appeared he had taken a liking to Miss Bessie's elixir.

I grunted.

She poured another shot.

With Buford's encouragement, I gulped it down, this time with better success. It didn't take long before I felt warmth extending out from the center of my body.

I relaxed.

Miss Bessie held my watery-eyed gaze with a devilish twinkle in her eyes. "Seems to me, Preacher, you have two choices. Either you get your voice, or one of us will have to do the speaking for you. You choose."

Her crossed arms and her firm stance told me she wasn't kidding. Knowing Buford's short history with Iris, my future bride, I knew he'd probably say the vows with a bit too much meaning than was necessary.

I nodded to Miss Bessie.

"Good. Now run along and get ready while I tidy up a bit. And don't you worry. I'll explain everything and say your vows as if I were saying them to you." An impish glint flashed in her eyes.

That got me worried.

Over the last two years, our relationship had grown. She considered me her best friend, probably because she'd outlived all her other friends. Being in the ministry, I found it hard to develop close friendships. With the exception of Miss Bessie, I too had no one else to call my friend.

Buford didn't count.

Definitely not Buford.

As I wobbled to my bedroom, I caught a glimpse of Buford topping off his third cup … or was it his fifth … who's counting? All I knew was that I had to regain my voice … and lost my equilibrium.

While in the shower, my head began to clear and to my surprise, I felt a tingling in my throat. Tentatively, I tried to hum. Something other than a frog-croak came out. It wasn't much, but it was more than I had all day. I continued to hum in an attempt at stretching out my larynx enough to squeak out an, "I do."

I towel dried my hair and tried to shave. After nicking my chin, I gave up and put on the rented tux. Stepping from my bedroom, I was surprised to find Buford dressed to the nines and Miss Bessie looking like she'd won the Miss Senior Georgia Pageant. She wore a sedate dress with a Victorian broach attached to her collar near her throat. A flossy hat sat precariously on her tightly wound hair.

Within a few minutes, Buford got the three of us safely to the church where the wedding party waited. Ignoring their questioning looks, I took my place down front.

Miss Bessie sat close.

Buford sat closer.

He grinned.

I wondered …

And prayed.

Still feeling the effects of Miss Bessie's elixir, I steadied myself on the front pew.

The music began and within moments, my bride-to-be descended the aisle. I was still a bit tipsy and wondered if I lost count on how many shots Miss Bessie poured into me.

Somewhere in the background, I heard my name and blinked back the fog. It was my turn to speak.

Miss Bessie cleared her throat, but before she could speak, I blurted, "I do," to whatever question the pastor asked.

Iris's eyes widened, then watered.

Hand to her mouth, she tried to inhale. It suddenly occurred to me.

My breath was laced with alcohol.

Chapter Eighteen

The Thieves

The phone next to my bed rang jolting me and Iris from a deep sleep.

It was the first week home, since returning from our honeymoon, and I was loath to wake up. Since returning, I'd officiated in an ordination service for a college friend in Statesboro. The following day, I assisted with another friend's wedding in the north Georgia town of Ellijay and then spoke at Reinhardt University's baccalaureate service. That service had been postponed due to weather, and the keynote speaker couldn't rearrange his schedule. Thus, I had to come up with a speech on the fly.

That being said, the moment my head hit the pillow, I was asleep. My week's activities seemed to have melded into a cocktail of mental scraps. I saw myself conducting the wedding of my friend, but rather than him reciting his vows, he was stating his position on the inerrancy of scripture; instead of him wearing a tux, he was wearing a cap and gown. It all seemed so confusing, and I was glad it ended as I could only imagine where he and his bride-to-be might have ended up on their honeymoon had my dream continued.

I groggily answered the phone trying not to disturb my wife … it didn't work.

"Hello?" I hoped it wasn't my mother … or my mother-in-law.

"Preacher? I've been robbed."

Miss Bessie's raggedy voice was fraught with anxiety.

"Are you all right? I mean, you weren't injured, were you?"

"No, Preacher, but you might want to come out here."

A thousand scenarios blazed across my mind. *Was she being held hostage? Was her house ransacked? Were the police there and she needed my council?*

Unable to satisfy my wife's questions, I stumbled from the bed in search of something to wear. "I'll be right there," I said breathlessly, hanging up the phone.

After a few minutes, I found a pair of jeans and slipped them on. I donned a tee-shirt and pushed my feet into my tennis shoes. Before racing out the door, I gave my wife a quick kiss. She offered to go with me, but I assured her I'd call if I needed her. Then I grabbed my New Testament and left.

Twenty minutes later, I skidded to a halt next to the old oak tree where I often parked. The gentle sunlight seeped through the leaves, illuminating a line of yellow police tape, which sagged in the morning air. I lifted it and dashed across the barren yard toward her house, which, by now, had every light on.

Bounding up the rickety steps, I burst into the house expecting the worst. Instead, I found the dear woman sitting calmly on her sofa with an officer kneeling in front of her. If this was any other circumstance, I would have thought he was praying, but I knew that wasn't the case. His earnest expression told me he was doing serious police business.

At the moment, she was giving the officer a detailed description of the events which led me and the policeman there.

She sniffed back a tear and spoke in a shaky voice, "I heard a noise in the front room, Officer, and feared for my life. You see, I've had a number of disturbances recently."

He waited.

So did I.

She continued. "I grabbed my shotgun and prepared to defend myself. Officer, I swear, I'd never hurt a flea if it didn't bother me first."

I knew from past experiences involving Miss Bessie and her shotgun, what kind of damage she could do. Once she took out the entire chicken population in her chicken coop when Ole Blue, her mangy hound dog, cold-nosed her. The other time was when she had a run-in with a skunk. I shuddered at the memory.

She feigned another sniffle and winked at me.

It was at that moment I knew something was up. There were no bloodstains or body parts lying around, so I knew whoever she shot at must have been outside. But even then, the ground in front of her house didn't look disturbed.

I continued to listen as she added to her statement.

The officer scribbled a note.

"As I eased my bedroom door open, which I always keep closed, I heard some scuffling and voices."

"What did they say?" The officer and I asked in unison.

"Well, I'm not exactly sure." She lifted her bony hand and stroked her furrowed brow. "It was in Spanish, I think. Whatever it was, it didn't sound like they were from these parts."

I smiled at her description of outsiders. As far as the community was concerned, I wasn't from these parts either.

"So what happened when you opened the door?" The officer asked.

Miss Bessie glanced at him, then at me. "Do I need a lawyer?"

Her question took me back for a moment.

"No, Miss Bessie," the policeman stated flatly, "you were in your home, defending yourself. If anything, it's the perpetrators who would need a lawyer."

Her expression darkened. "Well, I wasn't exactly *in* my house. When I opened the door, they skedaddled. I chased them out of the house and shot at them two peckerwoods as soon as I could."

I smiled.

So did the officer.

"Where exactly were you when you shot at them, Miss Bessie?"

She shifted in her seat and peered at me as if she wanted me to save her from the consequences of her actions.

"They'd nearly made it to the crick down the way," she said triumphantly. "I got a bead on them and squeezed off two shots before they climbed the fence. Hit 'em right in their backsides with a load of salt rocks."

I felt the blood drain from my face. The practice of swapping pellets for rock salt in a 12 gauge shotgun shell was a common practice for home defenders. It wouldn't kill a person, but it sure would make the intruder think twice before breaking into anyone else's house.

I found myself breathing again after a few minutes.

The officer stood and jotted something on his notepad. After inspecting the pump action shotgun, he leaned it against the wall. "And you say they only got away with a few items?"

She nodded. "Yes, but I found them on the other side of the

bob-wire fence."

The officer held up his hands. "Whoa! Are you saying you climbed over the fence?"

She nodded.

I held my breath.

I knew she was one spry bird, but climbing a barbed wire fence in the middle of the night in pursuit of two thugs must be a record.

"Yep," she continued, clearly enjoying the moment. "I followed their yelps until I lost them in the holler."

She glanced at me as she finished her statement, and I wondered what she wasn't saying.

"Is there anything else you remember?" By now, the officer was walking around looking for any clues the thieves might have left behind.

She shook her head and gave me a Mona Lisa smile.

"Well, I'll call in an APB and alert the local hospitals to be on the lookout for anyone with wounds consistent with a gunshot."

As she thanked him and walked him to the door, I sat quietly waiting for her to return, and tell me the truth.

I'd never known Miss Bessie to lie, but something in her narrative didn't pass the sniff test.

Taking her seat, she eyed me with an impish twinkle.

"Well, what really happened?" I asked, a slight tremble in my voice.

She rose and guided me back outside to the woodshed.

She tugged the handle and the door groaned as she swung it open. There, in the shadows stood a couple of teen boys. Their feet were tied. Their hands were bound behind their backs with an old rope. It was clear, they'd been scared spitless as evidenced by their wet pants and white faces.

"Preacher, I caught these two hoodlums outside before they did any damage. My shots went wild or I might have hurt them. Someone must have heard the shooting and called the police. I was able to tie them up and get them out here before the cop showed up."

"Why didn't you just turn them over to the policeman instead of holding them out here?" I asked, peering into the moonlit shed.

She gave me one of the looks she'd reserved for special moments and she tugged a thin cord. The single light bulb sprang to life and cast its yellow light across the room. Standing in the center of the woodshed were a couple of teenagers from my youth department. As a matter of fact, they were the only teens in my church. Immediately, I understood.

"Preacher, I think it's time for you to do a little discipling. You might start with teaching them the eighth commandment."

I pulled my New Testament from my back pocket and began

thumbing through it.

"It's in the Old Testament," she said, under her breath.

I felt my face redden. "I knew that. I was just looking for the New Testament interpretation of that verse."

She nodded. "Good, then it's settled. You three do a Bible study while I fix y'all some breakfast."

With that, she spun on her heels and padded into the house.

Chapter Nineteen

Miss Bessie's New Car

I had just dropped Iris off at the bank where she worked as a Teller. My meager salary was sufficient for me, but feeding two mouths required more than the church could afford. It had been a point of controversy which was settled only when Iris suggested she work outside the home. We knew going into our marriage would stretch us. I just didn't know it would be this soon.

Iris' father cautioned us about the dangers of marrying without proper financial planning. He meant well, but we were in love and figured two could live cheaper than one. We quickly learned how faulty that thinking was.

Fortunately, the bank had an opening and offered Iris the job. I felt there was someone behind the scenes, manipulating the circumstances … God, Reverend Ashcroft, Miss Bessie. I wouldn't put it past her.

As I chugged along the street, I realized how desperately we needed a newer vehicle. Iris had sold her's to purchase the wedding gown and pay for her bridesmaid's dresses, citing mine was in better shape than her's. That was until my mechanic, Miss Bessie's nephew, Buford, did an oil change and failed to tighten the oil pan plug. That oversight began the rapid decline on my engine's life.

Nursing my clunker along the main street, I noticed a pair of white knuckles gripping the steering wheel of a late model sedan. It was sitting at what once was a red light, and other cars were lining up behind it.

As I passed it going the opposite way, I got the distinct impression I'd seen that straw hat before. It suddenly dawned on me who it was behind the wheel. It was Miss Bessie. What was she doing? She doesn't own a car, let alone know how to drive, I thought. Or at least that is what the cagy old gal had led me to believe.

I made a U-turn and came up beside her as she sat at the red light. After indicating that she roll down her window, I waited until she could hear me. "Miss Bessie, what in Heaven's name are you doing? You're going to get yourself killed."

Her eyes took on an impish glint. "Isn't this the grandest thing? Everyone is so friendly; waving their hands and honking at me. I've always wanted to learn to drive. I figured if I'm ever going to learn, I'd better get with it. I'm not getting any younger. Anyway, it's on my bucket list."

"Your what?" I asked, as a logging truck barreled through the intersection.

Once the wind, dust and debris settled, I got out of my car and came around to her window. The experience of seeing that monstrous truck rumble past left the elderly woman badly shaken. Lips trembling, she said. "That was frightful. Would you mind teaching me how to drive? I feel like such a klutz."

Miss Bessie may have been many things, but a klutz was not one of them. After parking my car in Ace Hardware's parking lot, I returned to find Miss Bessie sitting in the passenger seat with her seatbelt snugly attached and a weak smile tugging at the corners of her mouth.

"You could have followed me into the parking lot," I said, trying not to sound too frustrated.

"Yes, but I was so shaken, I couldn't figure out which peddle I should push, so I gave up."

A silver tear caught a golden ray of sunlight as it slid silently down her cheek. My heart broke for the dear woman. She was not one to cry … not unless it worked in her favor.

I took a hard swallow. "Miss Bessie, how did you get this car in the first place?"

She tugged a Kleenex from her purse, dabbed her eyes and took a shuddering breath. "It's Buford's actually. He won it."

I felt there was more to the story, but someone behind us honked their horn. It didn't sound so friendly. Putting the car in gear, I pulled into the parking lot next to my car.

"He won it?"

Her face softened and she nodded her head. "Yes … playing poker."

My heart dropped like a felled tree. "I thought he'd given up gambling." That and drinking, chasing girls and a host of other vices, I thought but didn't say. He had made a profession of faith a few months ago and I thought he was making some progress.

As if she'd read my mind, Miss Bessie said, "He promised me this was the last time; that he'd truly given it up. The boy means well, but he's weak. Pray for him."

I had, but apparently not enough. "That explains how he got the car, but how did you get it?"

Her arthritic hand shot up stopping me. "Now, Preacher, don't go jumping to conclusions. He means well. He feels very bad about messing up your engine and thought this might set the record right. Plus, with your old clunker on its last leg, he figured if he gave it to me, I could give it to you. That way you wouldn't actually be benefiting from ill-gotten gain. You know how the deacons feel about gambling."

Yes, I knew how they felt about gambling. I also knew many of them played the lottery. One of them actually told me that if he ever won the lottery he'd be sure to tithe on it, after taxes of course. He had the audacity of quoting the verse, 'Give unto Caesar what is Caesar's and unto God what is God's.'

The following Sunday, I just so happened to preach from that passage. The following week I got a letter from my regional director warning me not to choose such controversial topics to preach on. I felt like I'd been sent to the principal's office for talking out of turn.

"Don't let them bully you," I heard Miss Bessie saying.

She must have read my mind.

"Yes, ma'am. Now about this car; do you want me to teach you how to drive or would you rather I take you home?"

With her finger to her chin, she feigned contemplation. "I think I'd like to learn to drive. But you must promise not to get frustrated. It's hard to teach an old dog, new tricks."

When it came to tricks, Miss Bessie was full of them. I wouldn't be surprised if she didn't already know how to drive. I knew not to ask to see her driver's license.

Crossing my heart, I promised not to get frustrated.

After exchanging positions, we spent the next forty-five minutes maneuvering around parked cars and driving down the back streets of town. She had an uncanny knack for driving; I had to admit and wondered if all that talk about being an old dog was just a ruse.

"What say we take her out on the four-lane and see what she can do," Miss Bessie said, her face beaming with anticipation. Pointing the car in the direction of the highway, she headed for the four-lane.

I started to protest when she gunned the engine and off we went. Gripping the steering wheel with dogged determination, she pressed the accelerator until we reached the posted speed. I had to admit, the car glided over the pavement like a cloud across the sky. With the windows rolled up and the air conditioning on, I couldn't hear the wind rushing past us.

"She sure rides good," I said, watching the speedometer creep higher. "Maybe we should keep it at 70 miles an hour. I wouldn't want you to get a ticket."

No sooner had the words left my lips, than a set of blue lights and a siren jerked my head around.

Miss Bessie muttered something unintelligible.

I didn't ask her to repeat it.

Turning on the tears, she proceeded to sweet talk the young officer. Amazingly and to my utter surprise … it worked. She got off with just a warning.

Once the ordeal was over, she turned to me and said,

"Preacher, would you mind taking me home? I think I've had enough excitement for the day."

I had to agree. It was pretty exciting. But I needed to get back to the office. I just hoped word didn't get back to the deacons about our little excursion.

As we pulled onto the gravel road leading back to Miss Bessie's home, she withdrew an envelope from her purse and pushed it in my direction. "This is the title and registration. The car is yours."

Hands raised, I tried to protest, but that was useless. Once Miss Bessie had her mind made up, there was no reasoning with her. Plus, Iris and I had been praying for one. With mine on its last leg, thanks to Buford's efforts, I extended my hand and took the proffered documents.

"Thank you, Miss Bessie. I will put this car to God's use as well as my family's."

"Good," she said, stepping out of the car. Leaning down to look me in the eyes, she continued, "I was hoping you'd say that. I have some ideas as to how God might put it to use."

I felt my heart tick up a notch, but before I had time to ask her to elaborate, she strode to her front porch.

"I'll be calling," she said over her shoulder.

I knew it wouldn't be long.

Chapter Twenty

The Bucket List

Standing in the front yard of my newly acquired parsonage, I inhaled the air and let it out slowly. It was laden with the scent of fresh cut hay. The dog days of summer were a distant memory, replaced by the spectacular colors of autumn.

This would be mine and Iris's first year to celebrate Thanksgiving, Christmas and New Year's together and I looked forward to creating our own memories and traditions, that a quiver full of little Iris's and Timothy's.

My church seemed to be plodding along, neither growing numerically nor shrinking, which is saying a lot considering the day and age we live in. Yet I hoped, after all the effort I'd put into the work to see some forward progress. I guess unity among the brethren was the best I could hope for.

Yes, I longed for the change autumn would bring, I mused as I sauntered to my office in the back of the church. I thought about taking my new car, but decided against it.

As to my spiritual life, I had reached a plateau. For the last two years of my pastorate, I'd learned to study the Bible and do a fair exegesis of scripture. I'd memorized large portions of the Bible and spent time praying for my flock, but even still; I felt I was getting nowhere. The thought of taking an online Bible course tickled the fringes of my mind. Though I wasn't a bad student in college, neither was I an 'A' student. The notion of voluntarily going back to school made my hands sweat. For a brief moment, I even considered the idea that God was finished with me here, but then the phone rang. As long as the people of this community needed me, I needed to stay. Looking at the caller ID, I knew immediately who it was … so much for praying and meditating.

"Hello, Miss Bessie."

"Preacher, how did you know it was me?"

It never ceased to amaze me how simple things as caller ID mystified the elderly woman.

"Miss Bessie, I got a new phone system, and it tells me who is calling before I answer it."

A huff filled the connection. "Well, how does it know? Does your phone know everyone in the county?"

I knew where this was going so I skipped the explanation and cut to the chase. "I s'pose so, Miss Bessie. How can I help you today?"

Another huff. "Preacher, I've been feeling like it's time …"

My heart sank. I knew the grand matron of our church wouldn't live forever, that one day she would pass on to her reward, but I'd hoped she'd stay around at least through the end of the year. Then again, I knew she was given to the dramatic.

"Time for what, Miss Bessie?"

"Time to move on, you know to get on with my life."

"Miss Bessie, I'd say you've gotten on with your life pretty well. Just think of all you've ..."

"No, Preacher, there's still some things on my bucket list I want to do. Things that won't get done if I don't get doin' them."

The feeling that I had just been set up wrapped itself around me like an old horse blanket. "Miss Bessie I heard you say something about having a bucket list, but I've got no idea what you mean."

"Yep, I've got one." Her gravelly voice took on a dreamy tone. "But I 'spect it's a bit rusty. Most of the things I'd kept in the bucket have fallen through the bottom, but there is still one thing in it."

I chuckled at her mixed metaphor. "Miss Bessie, bucket lists are not actually buckets—"

"Mine is," she corrected, "I've got a bucket," she tapped the phone against it making my ears ring, "Ya hear that? It's had newspaper clippings, magazine articles and prayer lists I've collected down through the years, so don't go tellin' me what I do or don't have." She didn't sound angry, just emphatic.

"Okay, Miss Bessie, so you have a bucket and a bucket list. What is in your bucket that you think it's time to do?" Even as I asked, I knew I would probably regret it.

"I want to go on a fast."

"A fast," I repeated rather half-heartedly. "Miss Bessie, are you sure you're up to that? I mean physically."

Another huff. "I'll have you know, Preacher, a fast is actually good for the body and good for the soul. Anyway, I feel I'm missing something *spititually.* No reflection on you or your preachin'."

Though she didn't mean it as an insult, I took the observation with a measure of self-incrimination. Partly because it was true and partly because I wondered how many other church members felt the same way.

"Miss Bessie, you don't have to go anywhere to go on a fast. You can stay home and do your fasting and praying in secret just as the Bible says."

Silence filled the connection, and I could almost hear the wheels turning in Miss Bessie's head.

"But didn't our Lord go to the mountains to pray? I thought it would be so wonderful to go to the top of a mountain and commune with God." Again, that same dreamy tone invaded her voice and I could see her eyes glistening, her face radiating. If we were in church, I'm pretty sure I would have heard her shout, 'Praise the Lord.' I felt guilty for trying to dissuade her. Truth be known, I needed to draw nearer to the Lord as well.

"Okay, Miss Bessie, where do you want to go?"

"I was thinking about Stone Mountain, you know, we could make it sort of a pilgrimage." She blurted without missing a beat.

"A pilgrimage?" I shot back before I could stop myself. If I had a bucket list, which I didn't, but if I did, that certainly would not be on it. "Miss Bessie, that would be an expensive and taxing journey. Are you sure you are up to it?"

Another huff. "Preacher, I've been saving up my tith—, eh, I've come into some extra funds and I think I can afford it. Anyway, it's not that far."

A wash of mixed emotions swept over me. I heard her place the bucket back on the floor before she returned to the phone. A crinkly sound followed and I could only guess she was opening a map. "I've studied the map and by my reckoning, it's only about one hundred ninety miles, should take about three hours to get there."

Not wanting to dampen her spirits, I had to offer my advice. "Miss Bessie, I've been to Atlanta. The traffic around the city is terrible. With the construction of the new stadium, a drive around the city could take hours."

"Good, that would give us plenty of time to fast and pray."

I felt like saying you fast and pray, but then that would sound like I was volunteering, not to mention very spiritual. I started to suggest her nephew Buford take her when I heard her saying, "One night on Stone Mountain should just about do it and we can get back to normal."

I didn't say it, but I thought normal was what we were trying to avoid. "Tell you what, Miss Bessie, if your doctor gives you a clean bill of health, that you can go on a fast and be gone for a day, then I'll drive you to Stone Mountain."

"Already done that."

"You've—"

"Yep, talked to Dr. Carmichael and he said I'm clear to go on a fast, just not too fast." She chuckled hoarsely at her own joke.

"Uh, Miss Bessie, that's not exactly what I meant. Did you tell him it was a fast and a long drive, that it might involve some walking?"

"Uh, well—"

"That's what I thought," I said triumphantly. "Maybe I should follow up—"

"Now Preacher, don't go meddlin' between a doctor and his patient. I'm as fit as a fiddle and you know it. Now, I've already made arrangements. I'll pay for the gas, the hotel rooms, and the tickets. You just get me to that mountain."

By now, Miss Bessie's insurmountable energy and enthusiasm had worn me down. "All right, Miss Bessie, I'll call Iris and let her know to pack for a day-trip."

"Already taken care of."

I feared to ask what she'd told Iris. I just hoped it wasn't too big a whopper. Maybe Miss Bessie needed a closer walk with the Lord after all. In the background of my musings, I heard her saying something about tomorrow around six o'clock in the morning. Still reeling from the shock of being lassoed into going half-way across the state with an elderly woman to see Stone Mountain, I hung up and leaned back in my chair. It squeaked like tortured mice and I stopped myself before the rickety chair gave completely out.

Maybe it was time for me to start my own bucket list, beginning with a new office chair.

Chapter Twenty-One

On to Stone Mountain, GA.

The following day, Iris and I arrived at Miss Bessie's house before the sun thought about visiting its rays upon this weary world. Long, inky shadows gripped the garden alongside her house. A heavy fog crept into the holler like the gray-clad ghosts of the Confederates making one last desperate charge before fading into the past. Even still, there was a peace which had settled around the tired old house. Suddenly, I envied Miss Bessie's little slice of heaven with her fog, and her ghosts, and her memories.

Standing on the porch was Miss Bessie. Ensconced in her finest Sunday go-to-meeting' dress, she looked like she owned the world. After giving me a slight nod, she shifted her parasol from one arm to the other and with a gloved hand, adjusted the flowery straw hat which sat precariously on her head.

"You look chipper," I said, as I got out of my car and came around to offer her assistance. A pert smile tugged at the corners of her mouth as she greeted Iris. "I'm so glad you decided to come along ... you know how people talk."

Iris smiled and waved the comment aside. She was well aware of how vicious a loose tongue could be. "I'm looking forward to spending time with you, Miss Bessie. Timothy has told me so much about you, I feel I practically know you."

Miss Bessie's eyes held a quizzical expression and I wondered if that was a good thing or not.

Finally, she broke the uncomfortable silence. "Thank you. Now, Preacher, could you get my bags? They're a trifle heavy."

Both Iris and I shifted our gaze to the porch where a large suitcase and a lumpy grocery sack sat. "Miss Bessie, what is in that grocery sack?" I asked, eyeing the brown bag bulging with an assortment of fruits and snacks. All no, no's for a fast.

"Miss Bessie, I thought we were fasting, not feasting."

She tipped her head upwardly. A pair of doe eyes gazed innocently back at me. Moonlight illuminated her face and I was struck by how angelic her features were. Despite what time and trials had stolen, she was still a beautiful woman. An impish twinkle sparkled in her eyes and I knew behind them lived a child yearning for adventure, to see beyond her mundane world, to experience one last dash into the unknown.

"Fasting is for those with burdens to bear. Today, we feast. Anyway, the doctor told me I needed to take my meds and it says clearly on the prescription, 'take with food,'. You wouldn't want me to go against the doctor's orders. Now would you?"

Feeling out-foxed, I lifted the suitcase and nodded to Iris to hand me the bag of groceries. When she drew close, I whispered, "Welcome to Miss Bessie's world."

She nodded, knowingly.

Who was I to take that away from this dear saint? Fast or feast, mountain or no mountain, this was going to be a quest for the record books … one that Iris and I will tell our children and grandchildren. This was our adventure and we were going to live it to the fullest.

Once we'd reached the four-lane, Miss Bessie's chatter filled the time as we watched the sun mount a victorious conquest of the morning. She chirped on about the beauty of the Indian Summer, the radiant colors, how the sunlight danced across the lakes and pond, the V-shaped geese flying south for the winter.

We munched our way across the state taking breaks at every Welcome Center to check the map and to admire the state's natural features. By the time we'd pushed through I-75 and the 285 rush hour traffic, it was getting near dusk. By the time we'd reached Stone Mountain Park, her excitement was palpable. We quickly found a parking place and got out. After stretching, Miss Bessie made a bee-line for the VIP ticketing where she secured three tickets for the show.

Upon returning, she breathlessly said, "If we hurry, we can take the last Sky Ride Cab Car to the top of the mountain."

Her energy abounded as Iris and I trudged behind her. "Yes, ma'am." Wishing I'd not had that last bottle of soda pop.

The atmosphere inside the cable car rang with excited children and nervous parents. None of which dampened Miss Bessie's spirit. She was a woman on a mission and she was nearing her goal. We arrived just as the sun began its slow descent around the curve of the earth. Taking a seat on a park bench, she sighed heavily and watched in silence as the golden orb escaped our view. A light breeze rose from below catching the brim of her hat nearly sending it heavenward. A quick move and she caught it before it blew away. She removed it, allowing a few strands of grizzled hair to blow wildly. She inhaled the sweet fragrance which the breeze carried along in its fingers and let it out slowly.

"It's beautiful," she whispered, not wanting to break the sacred moment. I had to agree.

A smile lit her face. "You know, one man's sunset is another man's sunrise."

It took me a moment to internalize. Aside from her wit, the woman possessed a depth of wisdom I lacked … and longed for.

She patted the bench and Iris and I joined her. Together, we watched the sun sink like a wounded ship. As its last golden rays faded from view, a park ranger interrupted my musings.

"Last call for the Sky Ride Cable Car."

I glanced up. Miss Bessie sat stock-still. "If we don't go now, we'll have to hike down the mountain in the dark."

She pried her eyes open and shifted. "I s'pose they don't allow camping on the mountain, do they?"

I shook my head. "No, I don't s'pose so." I was only slightly disappointed. A night on Stone Mountain would have been too cold for my liking.

We made it back to the seating area five minutes before the laser show began. After spreading out a large blanket, Miss Bessie rooted in the grocery sack and produced a bag of chips and assorted snacks which survived our journey. Then she plopped down and settled in for the display.

Like a child, she sat mesmerized while the green, red and blue strings of light etched out the outlines of three Confederate figures: Jefferson Davis, Robert E. Lee and Stonewall Jackson carved into the mountain. All at once, she gasped. Hands clasped in front of her chest, she sucked in a sharp breath as the figures began to ride their horses while "Dixie" played in the background.

Astonished, she leaned back, her eyes filled with wonder. "Only my Lord could do that," she said through an emotionally clogged throat.

I knew the truth, but who was I to ruin her moment. It suddenly dawned on me what this fast, this pilgrimage, was all about. Whether she knew it or not, she'd taught me a valuable lesson. She saw God in everything. It didn't matter if it was a man-made light show or a flock of geese flying in a V formation. She saw God's hand at work everywhere.

"I think I'm ready to go now." It was barely above a whisper, but I knew in my heart what she meant.

"How 'bout we find the hotel you reserved, get a good night's sleep and munch our way home tomorrow. She nodded sullenly as we sat in darkness.

Glancing heavenward, she pointed at the tiny specks glittering in the endless space. "They think they put on a show down here," she harrumphed. "Just think, Preacher, God puts on a magnificent light show every night, and we miss it 'cause we got our heads buried in the sand."

I followed her gaze. She was right, as usual. My perspective had been on the little things, the mundane things rather than on the God who sustains all things by the word of His power.

The following morning, we gathered for breakfast our faith renewed, our vision clear. For Miss Bessie, it was the completion of her bucket list. For me, it was the beginning of one.

As we approached the local hardware store, she leaned forward and touched my shoulder. Pointing to an empty parking slot, she said, "Pull in there."

Surprised at her abrupt change of tone, I glanced at Iris. She too wondered why the sudden change of plans. "Why are we stopping?" she asked.

Miss Bessie faced us, her eyes wide with expectation. "It's time to get a new bucket."

Chapter Twenty-Two

Upon Reflection

Glancing at the calendar, I realized it was forty years ago that we laid Miss Bessie Myers to rest. It had been years since I'd thought about her and her wacky, witty and wily ways. I took a few moments to reflect on our shared journey. In the years between my coming to Bethel Methodist Church and the present, I'd pastored many congregations, ministered to countless souls, both young and old, but none as interesting and insightful as Miss Bessie.

Her wisdom cut to the heart of the matter. No pretense, no hidden agenda, no ulterior motives, well, maybe a few, but never driven by selfish motives. It was mostly for my good and the expansion of the gospel. She left an indelible mark on my life, the life of her church and her community; it was only during her funeral that I'd learned to what extent.

Now that I'm retired from the pastorate, sitting under a young, green, seminary trained preacher-boy, I find myself wishing he had a Miss Bessie to mentor him. Heaven knows, he surely needs it.

I thought about the bucket ... the one Miss Bessie bought me the day we returned from Stone Mountain ... the one she insisted I take home and fill with dreams, desires, wishes, and prayers. It too had long ago rusted through, having been used as, what else ... a bucket. But that didn't stop me from dreaming, from desiring, from wishing and, of course, from praying.

My eyes found my bucket list. It lay folded on my kitchen counter. Lifting it shakily, I brought it close enough for my eyes to focus on its lines. They were worn and aged, but readable, although it didn't really matter. I knew the lines by heart. Many entries were lined out with a date, indicating they'd been achieved or answered. Somewhere near the bottom was an entry yet to be fulfilled; become a mentor.

Although I had counseled many young men over the years, I'd never actually mentored one. This new pastor, the young man fresh out of seminary seemed as good a candidate as any I'd met.

I knew I could do it.

I'd had a good trainer.

My only regret was my raggedy voice. Over the years, I'd damaged it to the point where it limited the length of my sermons. Anything longer than a twenty-minute sermon also drastically reduced my ability to continue. So I learned to restrict my messages to twenty minutes much to the delight of my congregation. The upside was that I had to hone my sermons to the least number of words with the biggest punch. No fat, no in-other-words, no misspeaks. However, the last time I spoke, left my vocal cords raw.

I picked up the rumpled business card with the pastor's number on it. It's raised gold-leaf letters had been rubbed smooth. I chuckled. What would Miss Bessie have said if I handed her a fancy business card with my phone number stenciled on it the first time I met her?

I dialed the number.

My raggedy voice sounded foreign to me, but I began, "Preacher, I was wondering if you could stop by. I've got some confessin' to do."

A soft chuckle echoed between the phones. It may have been a laugh, but without my hearing aides, I couldn't tell.

"Yes, I'll be happy to stop by on my way home."

The thirty minutes between my call and his arrival were spent drifting in and out of a fitful nap. Finally, light tapping on my nursing room door brought my eyelids up like a pair of blinds released by a mischievous child. It took a moment for my eyes to adjust and my foggy brain to chug to a start.

"Come in," I said.

A young preacher-boy poked his head around the door and

smiled.

I extended my hand and took his. He leaned down and kissed me on my cheek. I reached up absently and rubbed the place where his lips touched my unshaven flesh. His presence, the scent of his manly cologne, his nearness warmed my spirit.

"I recognize that cologne. Where'd you get it?" I asked.

He smiled broadly, "Don't you remember? You gave it to me last Christmas."

I shook my head. "Why would I have done that? I barely know you."

Something about the tilt of his head, the way he stood. His smile brought back a flood of memories.

"Granddaddy, we've covered this before. Now let me help you get to the dining room. Grammy will be getting worried."

"I knew that," I said, rubbing my forehead. It was a game we played. I'd act like I didn't remember who he is and he'd act like we'd known each other for years. At least that's the way it seemed.

The Chase Newton Series

by Bryan M. Powell

The Order

Follow investigative reporter Chase Newton as he goes undercover in search of the truth. What he finds puts him and those he cares for in mortal danger. Fast-paced and high- energy describes this first of three mystery and action thrillers.

The Oath

The president and vice president have been attacked. The vice president survived, but he is a hunted man. The man who was sworn in is an impostor and Chase must get a DNA from him to prove who the real president is.

The Outsider

After a thousand years of peace, the world is suddenly thrown into chaos as Satan is loosed from his prison. These action-packed stories will hold you breathless and capture your imagination until the exciting conclusion.

Bryan M. Powell

The Jared Russell Series

by Bryan M. Powell

Sisters of the Veil

Jared Russell, a former Marine turned architect, must navigate the minefield of hatred and prejudice to find the meaning of love and forgiveness.

ISBN - 978151057994

Power Play - #8 on Amazon Political Fiction

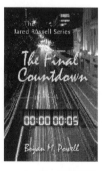

Jared and Fatemah Russell go Beirut, Lebanon, to establish the Harbor House, a refuge for converted Muslims and find themselves caught in a Middle East conflict of global proportions. ISBN – 9781511402750

The Final Countdown – #25 on Amazon

The clock is ticking and Jared once again finds himself battling against forces beyond his control. Can he and his friends unravel the mystery in time to stop two radical Muslims from perpetrating a horrible crime against our country? ISBN – 978153297825

Non-Fiction Series

by Bryan M. Powell

Seeing Jesus a Three Dimensional Look at Worship

Seeing Jesus is a thought providing and compelling expose' on what is true worship. ISBN -9781511540582

Show Us the Father

A thirty-day devotional showing how Jesus demonstrated His Father's character and qualities.

ISBN -9781517633905

Faith, Family, and a Lot of Hard Work

Born the year Stock-Market crashed, Mr. Gillis grew up in South Georgia with a 3rd grade education. After being challenged to get the best job in the company, he worked hard and got a degree from the University of Georgia and Moody Bible Institute in Finance. By mid-life, he owed 14 companies. ISBN -9781467580182

The Witch and the Wise Men

An ancient medallion is discovered,
An evil spirit is awakened,
A witch's curse is broken ... And
the wise men of Bethlehem are
called upon to face the ultimate evil

The Lost Medallion

Beneath the Hill of Endor is a
Temple, Inside the Temple is a
Chamber, Inside the Chamber is a
door, Behind the door ... the abyss.
And the key to the door is the
witch's medallion.

The Last Magi

Israel has signed the Peace Accord. The
Third Temple is under construction.
The world holds its breath as the Ark of
the Covenant is rediscovered, and then
stolen. It is up to the Magi to find it but
then what?

Journey to Edenstrae

What is the Tree of Life survived the
Flood and is living in a valley
guarded by a Dragon and a warring
people? 　　　　　　　　　～

Novelist Bryan M. Powell is a full-time author. Having worked in the ministry for over forty-two years, Bryan is uniquely qualified to write about Christian topics. His novels have been published by Tate Publishing, Lightening Source, Create Space, Kindle Direct Publishing and Vabella Publishing. His novel, The Witch and the Wise Men, held the #23 slot on Amazon's best seller's list and The Lost Medallion hit #22 on Amazon Christian Fantasy.

In addition to his novels, Bryan's short stories and other works appeared in *The North Georgia Writer* (PCWG's publication), *Relief Notes* (A Christian Authors Guild's book, released in 2014), and in the *Georgia Backroads* magazine.

Bryan is a member of the following organizations: American Christian Fiction Writers (ACFW), The Christian Author's Guild (President, 2016), The Paulding County Writers' Guild (PCWG), and the local chapter of ACFW, the New Life Writers Group.

www.facebook.com/authorbryanpowell
www.authorbryanpowell.wordpress.com
authorbryanpowell@gmail.com

Bryan M. Powell

Made in the USA
Columbia, SC
26 July 2019